BOOKSHOP NEAR THE COAST

BLUE HERON COTTAGES
BOOK THREE

KAY CORRELL

ZURA LU PUBLISHING LLC

ABOUT THE BOOK

Bookshop near the Coast

Collette owns the Beachside Bookshop in the charming town of Moonbeam. She's an avid reader and the shop is her dream come true. She has everything she's ever wanted or needed, right?

Mark comes to town for a highly suggested vacation. Okay, more like a vacation required by his boss after an incident at his workplace. An incident he feels is his fault.

He stays at Blue Heron Cottages and Collette befriends him. Wouldn't you know the one person he starts to like, owns a bookshop. Only… he's definitely not a book person. She's well-read, well-traveled, and so smart. He's… none of those.

Collette can tell that Mark is hiding something, but nothing she says or asks gets him to open up. His reaction to a horrible accident right in front of Sea Glass Cafe confirms her suspicions.

But Mark still won't talk and she's convinced there's no future for them if he can't be honest with her. And Mark isn't sure he can share his terrible secret.

Oh, and there's a wedding in the book, too. But who's getting married? One of your favorite couples!

Try book three in the Blue Heron Cottages Series

- Memories of the Beach - Book One
- Walks along the Shore - Book Two
- Bookshop near the Coast - Book Three
- Restaurant on the Wharf - Book Four (coming March 2023)
- And more to come!

Published by Zura Lu Publishing LLC

This book is dedicated to my brother who died way too young. He lived life to the fullest, was loved by many, and will be so missed. Rest In peace, Ken.

KAY'S BOOKS

Find more information on all my books at
kaycorrell.com

COMFORT CROSSING ~ THE SERIES
The Shop on Main - Book One
The Memory Box - Book Two
The Christmas Cottage - A Holiday Novella
(Book 2.5)
The Letter - Book Three
The Christmas Scarf - A Holiday Novella
(Book 3.5)
The Magnolia Cafe - Book Four
The Unexpected Wedding - Book Five

The Wedding in the Grove - (a crossover short

story between series - with Josephine and Paul from The Letter.)

LIGHTHOUSE POINT ~ THE SERIES
Wish Upon a Shell - Book One
Wedding on the Beach - Book Two
Love at the Lighthouse - Book Three
Cottage near the Point - Book Four
Return to the Island - Book Five
Bungalow by the Bay - Book Six
Christmas Comes to Lighthouse Point - Book Seven

CHARMING INN ~ Return to Lighthouse Point
One Simple Wish - Book One
Two of a Kind - Book Two
Three Little Things - Book Three
Four Short Weeks - Book Four
Five Years or So - Book Five
Six Hours Away - Book Six
Charming Christmas - Book Seven

SWEET RIVER ~ THE SERIES
A Dream to Believe in - Book One
A Memory to Cherish - Book Two

A Song to Remember - Book Three
A Time to Forgive - Book Four
A Summer of Secrets - Book Five
A Moment in the Moonlight - Book Six

MOONBEAM BAY ~ THE SERIES
The Parker Women - Book One
The Parker Cafe - Book Two
A Heather Parker Original - Book Three
The Parker Family Secret - Book Four
Grace Parker's Peach Pie - Book Five
The Perks of Being a Parker - Book Six

BLUE HERON COTTAGES ~ THE SERIES
Memories of the Beach - Book One
Walks along the Shore - Book Two
Bookshop near the Coast - January 10, 2023
Restaurant on the Wharf - March 2023
Plus more to come!

WIND CHIME BEACH ~ A stand-alone novel

INDIGO BAY ~ A multi-author sweet romance series

Sweet Days by the Bay - Kay's Complete
Collection of stories in the Indigo Bay series

Sign up for my newsletter at my website
kaycorrell.com to make sure you don't miss any
new releases or sales.

PROLOGUE

Three Months Earlier

Mark Wheeler grabbed a box from the stockroom and hauled it out into the front of Mason's Hardware Store. He carefully unpacked it, sorting through the items and placing them where they belonged. Neatly. In order.

He paused and rearranged a shelf a customer had obviously messed with. *He* never would have left it like that.

Why did customers do that? If they looked

at something but didn't buy it, couldn't they just put it right back where they found it?

He glanced at his watch. An hour until closing time.

Ian walked up to him. "Want me to finish that? Didn't you say you had a date tonight?"

The high school boy was fit and tanned and seemingly tireless. A good worker. They'd been lucky to hire him almost six months ago. The boy reminded him of himself at that age— which was more years ago than he liked to count.

Although Ian was the star quarterback for the high school team and Mark had never been a star anything. Summerville had a homecoming game this weekend against their biggest rival. Ian had talked of little else for the last few weeks. He was hoping some scouts would be at the game since he was still looking for a scholarship to college.

Mark glanced at his watch yet again. "I do have a date. But it's after work." He was ridiculously nervous about it. He couldn't remember the last time he had a date. This was someone his boss, Mr. Mason, had insisted on fixing him up with. Why did people do that? Try to find dates for him? He was perfectly happy with his life the way it was.

He'd arranged to meet the woman at the diner. It wasn't fancy, but a comfortable place for him. Which was exactly what he needed if he was going to have an actual date.

"No, really. Why don't you go home and get ready?" Ian hefted a box, set it on a shelf, and laughed. "I know, I know. Make sure I sort these out by size when I stock the shelf. Don't worry, I will."

He looked at his khaki slacks and shirt. The shirt had Mason's Hardware Store embroidered on the chest. He hadn't even thought of going home and changing. He'd just planned to go like this.

Ian eyed him. "Really. Go change."

"I guess I should. I'm pretty much off my game with dating." As if he'd ever been *on* his game with women.

"I can lock up."

"You sure?"

"I'm positive. We're not busy. I'll finish stocking the shelves and lock up at seven."

Ian was very responsible and had offered to close up before. And Mr. Mason had let him, so Mark knew it was okay. Still, it seemed irresponsible to leave early. He never left early.

Ian shook his head, grinning. "Go. Seriously. You need to change. Get out of your work clothes."

He held up his hands. "Okay, okay. I'm leaving. Don't forget to turn on the alarm."

"I won't."

Here he was, taking dating advice from a high schooler. Then again, Ian always seemed to have a girl on his arm, so he was probably exactly who Mark needed to listen to.

He quickly went home and put on navy slacks and a red knit shirt, then tugged off the red shirt and pulled on a white one. After slipping on loafers instead of the comfortable sneakers he wore to work, he debated shaving again. His heavy beard left a bit of a five o'clock shadow on his face. He glanced at the time and quickly ruled out the shave.

With one last look, he tamped down his nervousness and headed out to walk to the diner. Once inside, he greeted Marge, the waitress who had worked here forever, and took a table near the window. He only had the briefest description of his date. Tall, slender, blonde shoulder-length hair. Marge came over and he ordered a soda, explaining he was waiting for someone. She gave him a look of surprise but quickly hid it before heading off to retrieve his drink.

He sat at the table, glancing at anyone who walked past the window. A lone woman—but she had dark brown hair. A couple holding hands. The Ferguson family. He sat there for fifteen minutes.

Twenty. Thirty.

Marge came over. "Want to order?"

The heat of embarrassment crept over his cheeks. "Nah, I'm good. I think I'll head out now." He tossed some bills on the table. "Thanks, anyway."

He got up and strode out of the diner. It figured. He finally had a date, and she ghosted him. Just perfect.

What did you expect, Mark? Did you think someone would really be interested in going out with you?

He chased away the voice as a commotion down the street caught his attention. A frown crept across his mouth as sirens sounded in the distance. And was that the town police car with its lights flashing in front of the hardware store? His heart started hammering in his chest. He gulped a deep breath, then raced down the sidewalk toward the store.

CHAPTER 1

"Hey, Vi. Can you sit down for a minute?" Rob motioned to the kitchen chair.

"I'm kind of busy. Can it wait?" Violet eyed her brother. He looked... nervous? Guilty? What's up with that? She reluctantly sank onto the chair and stared up at her him, waiting.

He grabbed the chair across from her, spun it around, and sat down. He eyed her closely— never a good sign—and took a deep breath. "I have some news."

"And?" She cocked her head to one side, willing him to just get on with it.

"I found a place. I mean, a place to move to.

I bought a small cottage." He rested his forearms on the back of the chair. "But don't worry, it's not too far from here."

"You're moving out?" He'd been talking about it since… well, since he moved in with her to help restore the resort. But she'd gotten used to him being here all the time, even if he could be pretty annoying. Bossing her around. Always having an opinion on every little thing.

"You going to be okay living here alone?" He furrowed his brow.

"What? Of course. It will be nice to get you out from being underfoot all the time." She put on a brave smile. "It's about time."

He shook his head, and his eyes said he didn't believe her. He knew her too well. "I just need my own space. A place where Evelyn and I can go. A bit more privacy."

"Of course you do. A grown man can't live with his sister forever. And I don't need a babysitter, either." She rose from her chair, turned her back on him, and went over to the kitchen sink, surprised at how upset she was. She knew he wouldn't stay here forever, but still, as time went by, she'd gotten used to sharing the owner's suite with him.

He stood up. "I know you always act tough and say you can do it by yourself, but if you ever need my help, you know I'm here for you."

"And I'm there for you. Like when you'll have no idea how to furnish your new place." She still kept her back to him.

"Evelyn offered to help me with that."

"Oh." She swallowed her disappointment. Not that she really had free time to help him. She was busy with the resort. And she'd be busier now that he wouldn't be here. Thank goodness she had Aspen working here now.

"I've got to run. Meeting Evelyn at the cafe, then we're going over to Belle Island to the antique store. She said we'd probably be able to find some nice pieces of furniture there. But how about you and I have dinner tonight?"

"It's Friday. I have happy hour to run here at the cottages."

"That's right. I lost track of the days. Maybe tomorrow?"

"Sure. Maybe."

The chair squeaked behind her then she felt his hand on her shoulder. "You sure you're okay?"

"Of course. Why wouldn't I be?" She spun around and put on her best nonchalant look.

He nodded, his eyes skeptical. "Okay. I'll see you later." He walked out the back door and she sat back down on the chair. This would be okay. It would. She was used to being on her own. And hadn't her plan been to buy the resort and run it all by herself anyway?

He was just so darn handy with repairing things. And she'd miss chatting with him over coffee, and if she dared to admit it, she'd miss his teasing and the exasperating way he always had an opinion on every little thing.

But she couldn't blame him for wanting his own place and not sharing the owner's suite attached to the front office of the resort. A grown man should have his own place.

If only she didn't feel so deserted.

She jumped up. Enough feeling sorry for herself. She had happy hour to prepare for. As usual, she'd invited some people from town to come join her. The cottages were almost all full, so she should have a fairly good-sized crowd. She'd even run into the Jenkins twins and invited them. Jackie and Jillian. Though, she couldn't tell them apart. They'd been busy gossiping about a new shop scheduled to open on Magnolia Avenue near Parker's General Store. No one quite knew what was going into the new shop, but if anyone could find out, it would be the Jenkins twins.

She hurried out into the office. One more guest to check in. It was nice to have the cottages almost full for a week in this off-season month. She did love running the cottages. And she could do it without Rob's help. And his constant opinions. She could. And no way was she going to tell him how much she'd miss him…

Mark Wheeler stepped inside the office at Blue Heron Cottages. The air-conditioning was a welcome relief from the unusually hot day Florida was foisting upon its unsuspecting residents. Usually, by this time in September, the days had cooled off, at least a bit, after the rainy, humid summer.

A woman looked up from the desk and flashed him a warm, welcoming smile. "Good afternoon."

He stepped up to the desk. "Hi, I have a reservation. Mark Wheeler."

"Ah, yes, Mr. Wheeler. A two-week stay in the blue cottage." She checked him in and handed him a key. A real one, not one of those fancy keycard ones. Good. The keycards always seemed to make him fumble. Afraid he wouldn't work them right and get locked out. Not that he went out of town much to stay in a hotel, but still.

"I'm Violet, the owner. Glad to have you choose the cottages for your vacation."

He just nodded.

"We have a bookshelf over there if you want to borrow a book for your stay."

He glanced in the direction she motioned. He wouldn't be needing those.

"And the Wi-Fi password is Heron789. Capital H on heron."

He repeated the password three times, trying to remember it.

"But it's listed on a sheet on the counter in your cottage. There's a folder, too, of restaurants and shops. Oh, and there's a beach umbrella in the closet off the front room if you need one, and some beach chairs."

"Thank you, ma'am."

She smiled. "Just call me Violet. Everyone does."

"Thank you, Violet." She certainly was friendly and helpful. Maybe she'd have some idea of how he could fill his days for two entire weeks.

"Let me know if you need anything. Oh, and we have a free happy hour on Fridays. That's today. Be sure to come out and join us."

"Thank you. I will." He left the office, went to his car, and grabbed his suitcase. He'd picked up the suitcase from a thrift shop. It wasn't like he traveled around all the time. He couldn't remember the last time he'd traveled more than ten miles from home.

He still thought it was silly to be vacationing in Florida. Because he lived in Florida, so it wasn't really a vacation, was it? He'd only driven an hour or so to get to the beach. He lived inland in the small town of Summerville. The same small town he'd grown up in. Working a job at the same company he'd worked at since he graduated high school.

He climbed the stairs to the blue cottage, used the real key to open the door, and stepped inside. The interior was bright and cheerful, decorated in a beachy vibe. Not cluttered, though. He hated clutter. He liked things nice and organized.

He set the suitcase down and peered into the kitchen cabinets. Nicely set up with dishes and cookware. A coffeemaker and a bag of coffee. He'd go to the market and pick up a few items so he didn't have to go out to eat for every meal.

The resort was nicer than he'd expected. The buildings all looked freshly painted, and the air conditioner blasted out crisp, cool air. He was more of a fresh air kind of guy, but Florida didn't give him many chances to be that person.

Now if he could just relax and enjoy himself. On a vacation.

Vacation.

What did that mean, anyway? All he could think of was it was a couple weeks off work. And work was his routine. He liked routines. These weeks promised to be filled with... non-routine days.

But his boss had insisted he take the two weeks off. And get away. He couldn't remember the last time he'd taken more than a day off here and there.

Somehow he'd make it through this week and the next, and head back home. To his routine. To his job. To everything familiar.

Besides, he didn't think that two weeks could erase what had happened.

CHAPTER 2

Collette pulled the door closed to Beachside Bookshop and glanced at her watch. Four forty-five. She never left this early on a Friday, but she'd promised Violet she'd come to happy hour at the cottages. Violet had asked her numerous times, and she just couldn't stand to say she was too busy again. It sounded presumptuous. Wasn't everyone busy in their own way? Besides, she had Jody working at the shop. Jody could handle the Friday evening customers and close up.

Still, it was hard for her to leave. She took one last look at the bookshop and resolutely turned and headed down the sidewalk.

Her shop was at the corner of Magnolia and

Second. A corner location that she loved. She even had a covered courtyard out back where she offered up sweet tea and cookies on Saturdays, weather permitting.

She walked down the street, in no particular hurry, glancing at the shops lining Magnolia Avenue. When the weather was nicer, the shops would throw open their doors, and people would wander in and out. But today was a hot one and the shops had their doors closed and air conditioners blasting.

She loved the town of Moonbeam and counted her blessings that she'd found this town all those years ago when she was wandering around, trying to find a place to put down roots. When she found Moonbeam and a job at Beachside Bookshop, everything had fallen into place. She was an avid reader and loved working in the shop.

After a while, Mrs. Wetherby sold the shop to her, letting her pay it off over a ten-year period. Mrs. Wetherby said the shop could only go to someone who loved it as much as she did.

Collette was that person. She loved the little shop. She put in a reading corner for kids, expanded the selection of fiction books, and started selling gift items. After that, she put in a small coffee bar and added a couple of sofas and comfortable chairs scattered around the shop. Yes, she loved everything about it.

She continued her walk over to Blue Heron Cottages. And that was *another* thing she loved about Moonbeam. She could walk almost anywhere. And she did. A light breeze picked up, heralding the upcoming rain the weatherman had teased might hit later this weekend. That should break this heat, and hopefully the humidity would lessen. Soon they'd slip into October, bringing its cooler, perfect sunny days.

She crossed into the courtyard at the cottages and Violet waved to her from a table set up with wine bottles, glasses, and appetizers. A large washtub brimming with ice sat on the ground filled with beer and soda. Comfortable chairs strategically placed in small sitting areas dotted the courtyard. The fresh smell of gardenias wafted through the air from some random late blooms on scattered bushes surrounding the area.

Once again, she admired what Violet had done with the resort. Not the tired old cottages from when the prior owner, Murphy, had let it get so run down. The cheerfully painted cottages welcomed everyone. Each one had a nice front porch, complete with a ceiling fan and comfortable chairs. Just a really nice, quaint place to stay with an old Florida feel to it.

Violet greeted her as she walked up and gave her a quick hug. "I'm so glad you came."

"I am, too. Look at this. You've done such a great job with the resort."

"Thank you. There's still more work, but I'm pleased." Violet's eyes lit up at the compliment. "Would you like wine?"

"I would. White, please."

Violet poured her a glass and handed it to her. She took a sip of the crisp, cool wine, savoring the flavor.

Rose walked up to them. Rose had been staying at the cottages for a few weeks and had come into the bookshop frequently. They had many friendly chats, sharing their love of books.

"Rose, good evening." She greeted the woman. "That book you ordered came in this afternoon. I should have thought to bring it with me."

"Oh, it did? Great. I'll drop by and get it

tomorrow. Besides, I'd hate to miss your sweet tea and cookies."

Collette laughed. "It does seem to bring in the regulars, plus any other visitors to town who walk by and notice the sign outside."

Violet waved to a man coming out of the blue cottage. "Hey, Mr. Wheeler, come on over and join us."

She glanced across the distance at the man. He hesitated on the edge of the stairs, as if uncertain he wanted to join them.

Mark put on a smile and lifted a hand in a small wave to Violet. He wasn't much of a small talk and mingle kind of guy, but he was trying to force himself out of his comfort zone a bit with this trip. So he'd accepted Violet's invitation to happy hour. Even if standing around sipping a drink and talking to strangers was the last thing he wanted to do. What would he have to say to them? Situations like this made him feel awkward and out of place, so he tried to avoid them.

With a sigh, he stepped off the porch and

crossed the distance to the table Violet had set up in the courtyard. He hoped his smile looked friendly… even if it felt slightly pained to him.

"Mark, glad you joined us," Violet greeted him warmly. "This is Rose, another guest here at the cottages." She motioned to an older lady standing by the serving table.

"At this rate, I'm going to be a permanent guest." Rose laughed, her eyes twinkling with amusement. "I keep extending my stay."

"And you're welcome to stay as long as you want." Violet smiled at Rose, then turned to the other woman standing beside her. "And this is Collette."

"Nice to meet you." He nodded toward the two women and shifted from foot to foot, still wondering if his smile looked fake to everyone.

"What would you like to drink?" Violet asked, the consummate hostess.

He was pleased to use the word *consummate* in his thoughts. His boss had used it the other day, and Mark had no clue what it meant. After a few poor attempts to look it up online with wild guesses at spelling, he learned it described someone with a flair for something. At least he hoped that's what it meant. "I'll have a beer."

"Sure, choose what kind you like." She motioned to a washtub filled with beer and soda.

He plunged his hand into the frigid water, pulled out a beer, and twisted off the cap. He took a quick swig of it to fortify himself. Then his eyes locked with Collette's sky-blue ones. Smile lines framed them, and they sparkled when she smiled at him. He sucked another sip of beer as uneasiness gripped him in a firm hold. He glanced back at the safety of his cottage, wondering if he could make a quick escape.

"Mark is staying here at the cottages for a couple of weeks." Violet interrupted his escape as she poured a glass of red wine and handed it to Rose. She looked up and called out a greeting to another couple crossing the courtyard. "Melody. Ethan. Come on over."

Violet. Rose. Collette. Melody. Ethan. He repeated the names a few times to memorize them.

Violet made more introductions, then he and Collette stepped back as more people approached the table. Collette motioned to some chairs in the shade of a tree. "Want to sit?"

"Uh, sure." *Smooth, Mark. Very smooth.*

They crossed to the chairs and sat down. "So have you been to Moonbeam before?" Collette asked.

"No, first time."

"How do you like it?"

"Uh, I just got here this afternoon." *Don't say* uh *again!*

"If you're here for a few weeks, you'll have plenty of time to explore. We have a great wharf that extends out into the bay. Lots of restaurants and shops there and in town. Oh, and Delbert Hamilton bought the old Cabot Hotel and restored it. It's beautiful now. Well worth stopping in and taking a peek." She laughed. "Sorry, I sound like a tour guide."

"No, I appreciate the suggestions." He would have to figure out something to do to fill his time.

"The beach is beautiful here, too. Lots of good shelling."

He was embarrassed to admit he was a Florida native and had never gone shelling. He'd actually only been to the beach a handful of times, which was probably an embarrassment for a Floridian.

"I sound like the Moonbeam ambassador, but I love it here."

"Have you lived here long?"

"I have. About forty years."

Forty years ago. He glanced at her and tried to figure out her age. She had hints of gray at her temples and those smile lines by her eyes. But he was terrible at guessing women's ages. Maybe she was about his age? Maybe. He'd just turned fifty, and that still surprised him. Fifty years old. How had that happened? Wasn't he just the other day an awkward, out-of-place teenager? He laughed to himself. He was *still* awkward and out of place. Only the age had changed.

"So, what do you do? For a living I mean." Collette asked.

"I'm a manager at a hardware store."

"Oh, really?"

"I've worked there since I started as a stock boy when I was in high school. Worked my way up. I really enjoy it." Well, he used to enjoy it. Then he started having nightmares about it. But really, after what happened, who could blame him?

He changed the subject. "And how about you?"

"I own the bookshop in town. Beachside Bookshop."

The bookshop. It figured. The one person he was getting to know in town owned a *bookstore*. They couldn't be any more different if they tried. She was probably smart and knew a lot about everything. Book people were like that. He took a sip of his beer. "Uh, that sounds like an interesting way to make a living." *What a ridiculous thing to say. And what is up with all the* uhs*?*

"I love it. Love the shop. My customers. Finding new books to stock."

"Guess you read a lot, huh?" *Oh good, the* uhs *have changed to* huh.

"All the time. I either have a book with me or an e-reader loaded with books. I'm on a kick of reading travel books right now. Trying to plan my next trip. I take two weeks off each year, close the shop, and travel somewhere. Last year was Ireland. So gorgeous. The year before, I popped around Europe. Hit London, Paris, and Rome. I was thinking maybe a villa in Tuscany this year."

"Wow, you've been to a lot of places." He'd been to… Florida.

"Travel is kind of my thing. I've been to Belize, Croatia, Mexico, Canada, oh, and all over the United States. And planning the trips is as much fun to me as the actual trip."

The woman was getting more and more different from him as the evening progressed. He was embarrassed to admit he'd never even left the state. He liked his small town, his familiar places. He really had no desire to travel. Not even for this forced-on-him vacation.

"Do you travel much?" She peered over the rim of her wineglass.

"Uh, no. I don't travel much. Seems like I'm always working." Except for these two weeks, of course. The two weeks his boss had insisted he take. His boss's assistant had even booked the resort for him because Mr. Mason knew him too well. He'd never have taken the trouble to actually book the cottage. He would have sat in his house for two weeks.

"Oh, that's too bad. I mean, I work a lot. All the time, it seems. But I do take my two weeks off each year for my trips. Look forward to them all year long." She smiled at him again, making him feel a little less out of place. Like she was enjoying just sitting here chatting with him. "Anyway, enough about me. So, are you going to hit the beach tomorrow or go poke around the town?"

"Now that you've told me about some places here, I think I might go explore."

"If you come into town, you should stop by my shop. We have sweet tea and cookies on Saturday in the courtyard behind the shop."

"I just might do that." Imagine that. Mark Wheeler in a bookstore.

"And if you're an early riser, the sunrises are pretty. A bit of reflected sunrise over the water. And we throw some pretty spectacular sunsets."

"I'll remember that and try to catch one." By sunrise, he was usually already at work. And stayed after sunset quite often except for the summers when sunset was so late. But even then, he just headed home to eat his dinner alone. Or stopped at the diner to grab a sandwich. The diner where they knew his name and he could count on the meatloaf special every Tuesday evening and fried chicken on Thursdays.

Silence fell between them, and he shifted in his seat, wondering what to say, to ask. So far she'd been carrying the conversation. See, he was terrible at small talk.

"So, what do you like to read?" She interrupted the silence.

"I… I, uh… don't read much." The last book he could remember reading was a required book in high school English class.

She smiled. "I guess you don't have much time if you work so much. But while you're on vacation, you should stop by and see if you can find something interesting. Vacations are a great time to catch up on your reading."

"I should," he answered, not knowing what else to say. But reading was certainly not the way he wanted to spend his time.

"Good, then I look forward to seeing you tomorrow. Hope you stop by." She rose from her seat. "I should go chat with Melody and Ethan for a moment before I leave. It was nice meeting you."

He stood. "It was nice meeting you, too."

She smiled again, her eyes lighting up with

29

sincerity. She was a charming woman. Friendly. Outgoing.

The exact opposite of him.

She walked away, and he took the last sip of his beer. He looked around at the laughing, chatting people and slipped away, back to the safety of his cottage.

CHAPTER 3

The next morning, Mark woke up early. The whole day stretched before him. Most people would be excited to have long hours of relaxation beckoning them. But all he could think of was what in the world would he do? And two weeks of this. Maybe after a week, he could call his boss, say he was all rested up, and pop back home…

He got dressed and slipped outside. The sky was just beginning to lighten. A gentle breeze teased the palm branches, making them sway. He headed toward the beach, taking Collette up on her suggestion that he should try to catch a sunrise.

The older woman he'd met last night was sitting on the beach. What was her name? Rose. That was it. She waved to him and motioned him over. "Do you want to catch the sunrise with me? Pull up some beach."

It wasn't like he had any other plans. Though, small talk with a stranger wasn't his thing, either. He dropped down to the sand, unwilling to appear rude.

"I love coming out here in the early mornings. Not many people up. The birds are busy flying around, calling to each other. Some days there are waves, like today. I heard we're getting rain later. And some days the gulf looks as flat as a lake. It's an ever-changing view."

The waves rolled to shore in a slow march, and a trio of gulls flew past. The sky was tinged with a bit of pink. "It's nice out here," he admitted grudgingly. He wasn't used to just… sitting. The view was nice. But how long could a person sit and just… look?

"It is. My favorite time of the day. Though, I'm partial to the sunsets here, too. Watching the last bit of the day slip away."

"I'll have to catch a sunset while I'm here."

Everyone seemed to be about the sunrises and sunsets here in Moonbeam.

"Violet said you're here for two weeks." Rose laughed. "I was here for one week. Then extended my visit for another. Now I've been here a while and really have no desire to leave yet. Be careful. You never know how long Moonbeam will charm you into staying."

That wasn't going to happen.

"What in the world do you do all day?" His words spilled out before he could stop them. The heat of embarrassment crept across his cheeks. "I mean…"

An easy smile played at the corners of Rose's lips. "That's part of what I like about Moonbeam. A bit slower paced. Taking long walks. Catching the sunrise. I've even helped Violet at the resort. Each day I just get up and see what the day brings."

"No plans at all? No routine?"

"Nope. Oh, and I've been reading a bunch. I love to read."

Ah, another book reader. The town was full of them.

"So, what do you plan on doing with your time off?"

He shook his head. "I have absolutely no idea. I'm not really a vacation sort of guy. I like my routines. I like my days planned."

"Maybe you should try to just relax and see what each day has in store for you," she gently suggested.

He sent her a rueful look. "I'm not sure I know how to do that." It didn't sound very relaxing to him. But maybe he could make up a list of all the things he could see or do around town. Make a plan. A plan would help. Stick to it. Get some kind of routine going.

She patted his hand resting on the sand between them. "I think you should give it a try. You might be surprised. Maybe you'll enjoy yourself." She laughed. "It's hard to not enjoy yourself in Moonbeam."

He looked out at the water as beams of light filtered through the clouds and illuminated the waves. It was peaceful. Maybe he'd take her suggestion. Just see what each day brought.

Or he'd go back to his plan to make a list and do things in order. Group them by location. Try the wharf first. Or maybe downtown first. Get his days all organized. He wouldn't mind seeing Collette again. She'd been nice and friendly to him.

"You should go by the bookstore. Pick out some books to read for your stay. Collette has cookies and sweet tea on Saturdays. You should stop by," Rose said, unaware that she'd been reading his thoughts.

"That's what Collette said."

"I'm sure she can find you the perfect book to read. She has a special knack for that."

If Collette could find a book he wanted to read, she was indeed a miracle worker.

Rose watched Mark as he headed back to the cottages. He seemed like a nice young man. She smiled at her thoughts. Most people seemed young to her. He was probably in his late forties or early fifties. A bit pale, but this vacation would cure that.

There was something about him though. A loneliness or a standoffishness. Like he wasn't sure how to connect to people.

And she'd seen a brief second of panic when she suggested he go to the bookshop and pick out something to read. But then, some people were not readers—not that she'd ever understand that. Books could take you anywhere. Let you escape for a while.

Books had been her salvation after Emmett was… gone. She looked out at the sea with its waves rolling methodically to shore. Reassuring. Constant. How she loved this place, this view.

"Ah, Emmett. I miss you so much. It feels strange being here without you. And yet, it's so familiar that it's comforting."

She could talk to her husband here. Almost, *almost*, like she had so many times in the past. Only… very different. But she believed he still heard her words. Was here for her in some way. But oh, how her heart ached for him.

A sandpiper ran up the beach and stared at her for a moment before turning and racing back to the water's edge.

Enough melancholy. She pushed up off the sand. Time for more coffee. She'd head up to the office and say good morning to Violet. She'd fallen into a routine of coffee with Violet after watching the sunrise most mornings.

Violet was such a nice young woman. Friendly. Full of life and energy and laughter.

And the teasing between Violet and Rob. It made her smile. They were so close. Like siblings should be.

A momentary pang filtered through her.

Like siblings *should be…*

CHAPTER 4

Collette bustled around the shop the next morning, starting the coffee and straightening up stacks of books here or there. Precisely at nine, she flipped the sign in the window from closed to open. She placed a sign on the sidewalk near the door announcing it was sweet tea and cookies Saturday.

Soon the shop filled with a steady stream of customers. She looked up to see Emily Foster breeze in, all excited. "I got the email that said my book is in. I can't wait to read it."

Collette reached under the counter and pulled out the book on the history of Florida. The girl loved history and worked part-time at the history museum when not working at

Parker's General Store for her grandmother. "It looks like a good one. And lots of footnotes in the back. Might lead you to other research."

Emily took the book and opened it to the table of contents, her eyes running down the list. "Oh, I can't wait. I'm so glad you found this one and suggested it to me." She pulled out cash from her pocket and paid for the book. "Thanks so much, Collette. You're the best."

The girl twirled around and swept out of the shop. Collette grinned. Emily was filled with energy. She never seemed to just walk. She always was twirling or racing. Ah, to be that young again with your whole life stretching before you.

Though she had plenty of life enough ahead of her. Many plans of things she wanted to do. Places she wanted to see.

The day sped by, filled with regular customers and people visiting the town. She had to admit she was a bit disappointed Mark hadn't stopped by. She'd thought he might after she'd invited him. He'd looked a little lost at Violet's happy hour last night. She just wanted to make sure he felt welcome during his stay.

It started to darken outside, some from the

approaching evening and some from the promised rain. She peeked out the window and dark storm clouds, an ugly bruise color, gathered in the sky. Not a customer had come in during the last twenty minutes or so. Not surprising. Floridians knew to head inside when a storm like this was brewing.

She turned back to the counter to check on some orders when the bell jingled over the door. She looked up to see Mark step inside, looking every bit as uneasy as he had last night.

"Mark, welcome," she called out to him, motioning him over.

He crossed the distance and stood looking around, his hands jammed into his pockets. "Uh, your store. It's nice. Bigger than I thought."

"Thanks. I did clean out a large storeroom and expand the shop area into it. Made a kids' reading corner. Opened a coffee bar." She glanced out the window. "I was just going to head out to the courtyard to bring in the remains of the tea and cookies. Looks like this storm is going to hit any minute."

"It does. I wasn't sure I'd make it here before it hit."

"You can just browse around. I'll be back in a jiff."

"Here, let me help you."

He followed her outside, and she handed him a large tray with just a few cookies left. This week she'd gotten almond sandies from The Sweet Shoppe over on Belle Island. They'd obviously been a big hit. She grabbed the glass urn with a bit of tea left in it. They headed inside with their load, then back out to take off the tablecloth, close the sun umbrellas, and gather up a couple of trays of paper plates and cups. Just as they were finishing, large raindrops splattered onto the flagstone patio in the courtyard.

"Just in time." They raced inside. "Just set the tray over there on the coffee bar."

The sky opened up and rain poured down with such a vengeance she couldn't even see across the street when she peered out the window.

"Quite a storm." Mark walked up beside her.

"Florida is known for that."

"I know."

She turned to him. "Oh, have you been to Florida often?"

He laughed and gave her a rueful smile. "I live in Florida. Have all my life. Summerville. Only about an hour or so from here. Inland."

"Oh, really?" That surprised her. He just didn't look like a Florida native. He was pale and… but really? What was she thinking? Like a Florida native looked a certain way? Since when did she categorize people like that?

"Really." He nodded.

"You're used to our storms then." She turned from the window. "How about I find you a book to read while you're on vacation? What do you like to read?"

"I… I'm not sure. I don't read much."

"A local writer, Rob Bentley, has a new book out. It's really good. He's actually Violet's brother. Or there's another almost local author. He lives up in Wind Chime Beach, a bit north of here. Gabe Smith. Both are talented writers."

"You choose."

"Okay, let's start with Rob's newest. Then, when you finish that, we'll see if you like Gabe's."

~

Mark smiled weakly. "Sure, great." Not that he could imagine getting through one book, much less two, in his time here in Moonbeam. He was the slowest reader ever. You know, if he ever read. Which he only did when he had to. He'd buy the book and that would be that. Collette would be pleased, and he'd give it away when he got back home.

"After you read it, I'd love to talk to you about it." Collette smiled. "I have… thoughts." She laughed. "I always have thoughts and opinions about every book I read."

Now what would he do? Panic slowly crept through him. He could try to make his way through the book, but it would take him forever. To say he was a slow reader was like the world's biggest understatement. He hated to look not so smart to her.

"I listened to it on audio. Great narrator."

A smile slipped onto his face. That would work. He'd buy the book from Collette, then go back to his cottage and get it on audio and listen to it. She'd be none the wiser. Wonder how many hours it was on audio? Well, he had plenty of time to listen to it.

He bought the book and glanced over at the window. "Still coming down."

"It is. You can't go out in that."

He agreed with her on that. He'd be drenched within seconds. But Florida storms had a way of blowing through and ended as quickly as they came in.

"How about I close up the shop early? I can't imagine I'll have more customers with this storm."

"Oh, don't close up early on my account. Besides if you do that, I'd have to go out in this storm." He held up the book, pointing to the window.

"I thought I would invite you to my place."

He still thought they'd get soaked going to her place…

"I live upstairs above the shop."

"Oh." That explained it.

She walked over to the door, locked it, and flipped the sign to say closed. "Come on, follow me."

He followed her through a door in the back of the store, then up a steep flight of stairs. She opened another door, and they stepped inside. Full-length windows filled the wall overlooking the street. The walls were red brick, and an old wooden floor, weathered over the years, poked out around the many colorful scattered rugs. A kitchen with cherry cabinets and stainless appliances sat to one side.

"This is nice." He turned to her. "Really nice. I love the high ceilings." He glanced up to see a smattering of fans strategically placed along the ceiling. It was all one big room and very inviting. A long set of bookshelves ran the length of one wall. Of course. He would have expected no less.

"Mrs. Wetherby used to live here. That's who owned the shop before me. When she sold me the shop, she moved north to be by her kids. So I moved in here. Been here ever since."

The room was decorated simply. A small wooden table with four chairs near the kitchen. A couch and two overstuffed chairs centered in the room. A teal rug covered the middle of the floor and two lamps spilled soft golden light into the room.

She walked over and flipped a switch, and ceiling lights poured down light into the kitchen area. "How about a drink? I have some red wine or a few beers in the fridge."

"A beer sounds good."

She handed him a beer, taking one for herself. He wandered over to the bank of huge windows looking over the street. The streetlamps had come on, throwing small pools of light on the wet sidewalks. A roll of thunder sounded in the distance.

She walked up beside him. "I never tire of this. I often sit up here in the windowsill and just watch the world go by outside."

So different from his place. He lived in a small house on the edge of town. Very small. Two bedrooms, one bath. No view. But it was private and down a long country road. He liked his privacy. But he could see how a person would like a view like this. Sitting up above it all.

She turned. "Come. Let's sit."

He followed her over to the sitting area, and she sat on the couch. He took a seat on an overstuffed chair across from her and took a swig of his beer. Now, what should they talk about? Hopefully not books.

"So, two weeks off from your work. That's a nice break, isn't it? I find two weeks the perfect

47

vacation. Long enough to relax, but then I get anxious about the shop and I'm ready to head home."

"I don't know. I haven't ever taken two weeks off."

"Never?" She raised an eyebrow.

"No, I haven't even taken a full week off. Just a long weekend here and there."

She sighed. "That doesn't make for a very balanced life."

"I like my work," he said defensively.

"Oh, I didn't mean it like you're doing something wrong. I work a lot, too. It was more of a commentary on my life. I used to take my two weeks off, but nothing else. I work six days a week. The shop is closed on Mondays. But then I hired Jody and I try to take another day a week off. Jody suggested I take Tuesdays off, so I have two days off in a row. I don't always manage it—I really hate being away from the shop for two days in a row—but I try."

He relaxed a bit, realizing she wasn't criticizing him. "My boss nags at me to take more time, but I usually end up going in for at least part of the day on my days off. Mr. Mason —that's my boss—has given up on me taking time off." Except for this trip. This one was more than suggested. It was required. And set up for him. And paid for by Mr. Mason. And there was no way to refuse. It wasn't a suggestion at all.

But this was only his first full day in Moonbeam and he was worrying about the store. Did the order of sealer come in for Mr. Greenway so he could seal his deck this week like he wanted? Had Mr. Mason remembered to run the weekly reports at the end of the day on Saturday?

They were short of help now, too… And that was his fault.

He took a sip of his beer, ignoring the guilt threatening to crash through him.

"So, would you like a sandwich? I have leftover roasted chicken and I could make us a salad." Collette interrupted his thoughts.

"Oh, you don't have to do that."

"It's no trouble. Was going to have that for my dinner anyway and there's plenty." She got up and headed to the kitchen, rattling around and fixing their meal.

He got up and went over to the window again, looking down on the street. The rain was letting up a bit. Two kids splashed in the puddles at the edge of the sidewalk, their mother laughing at their antics and keeping a close eye on them. A woman hurried past, carrying an umbrella. A man walked along with his dog. Neither seemed bothered by the light rain.

"It's ready."

He turned and walked over to the table. She set it with colorful placemats and napkins, and a small bowl with a few flowers graced the center. Often he just ate standing at his sink. This was nice.

They sat down and he took a bite of the sandwich. "Oh, this is good."

"I can't take much credit. I got the roasted chicken from Parker's Cafe—I mean Sea Glass Cafe." She shrugged. "Hard to remember to call it Sea Glass. I always think of it as Parker's. The Parker family owns it and the general store in town. And I got the bread from over on Belle Island from The Sweet Shoppe when I picked up the cookies for today."

They finished their meal, and he helped Collette clear the table and do the dishes. It was comfortable just chatting a bit and doing the work. Not something he'd ever imagined himself doing. Chatting while doing dishes. And it strangely felt… natural.

Oh, he could talk to customers. There was always talk about their repair project, or advice on how to fix something, or his best suggestion when they were trying to choose between two options. Customers were easy. Other chatting? Not so much.

When they finished, Collette took out a plate and filled it with cookies. "I saved some. I love the cookies from The Sweet Shoppe, so I squirreled some away for me." She smiled as she led him back to the sitting area. He took his same seat, reached for a cookie, and took a bite.

"Oh, these are good." *Great. He was starting to repeat himself. At least it wasn't uh again.*

"They really are, aren't they?" Collette said as she reached for a cookie. "I sometimes bake the cookies for my Saturday cookies and sweet tea, but I didn't have time this week so ordered from Julie—she owns The Sweet Shoppe."

Silence drifted between them. What happened to his newly found ability to chat? He finished the cookie and stood, ready to escape the awkward silence. "I should probably go. I've taken enough of your time. And thank you for dinner."

"My pleasure." Collette rose and led him to the stairway and downstairs. She opened the back door.

The rain had ended, and a few stars peeked through the clouds.

"You know your way back?" she asked as he stepped outside.

"I do. And thank you. For dinner and the book suggestion." He held up the book.

"I hope you enjoy it."

As he headed around the building and out onto Magnolia, he glanced up and saw Collette in the window. She waved to him and he waved back. He turned and headed back to the cottages, eager to get online and find the audiobook for the paperback he'd gotten. Maybe he could even listen to some of it tonight. It wasn't like he had anything else to do.

The moon broke through the clouds and spattered light through the trees. More stars lit up the sky. The trees and bushes sparkled in the light with their freshly washed leaves.

It was a cute little town. No wonder Collette liked it so much. A couple passed by and smiled at him. A friendly town, too. Not that his hometown wasn't friendly—but the last few weeks people darted looks at him and whispered. Or at least it felt that way to him. Not that he really blamed them…

He pushed those thoughts away as he entered the courtyard of the cottages. Violet and Rose were sitting outside the office. "Hey, Mark," Violet called out.

"Evening." He called back and waved as he passed them. He continued to his cottage, unwilling to stop and have to deal with more social chat tonight. He'd done enough of that. Although, most of the night, it had been easy to talk to Collette. Until it wasn't. Until he'd gotten all tongue-tied and wrapped up in his thoughts. He never could quite get out of his thoughts these days.

He pushed inside, flipped on the light, and set the book down. He took out his phone and searched for the audio version of the book.

Success. He downloaded the book and hit play.

Soon he was engrossed in the story, hardly noticing the hours slipping by.

CHAPTER 5

The next morning Collette got up early, as usual, and unloaded the dishwasher from last night's dinner. She had a nice time with Mark last night. She'd surprised herself by inviting him up to her apartment. But she couldn't let him go out in that rainstorm, could she? She was just being neighborly and friendly.

There was something about him, but she wasn't sure what it was. But she'd enjoyed talking to him. And it had been a pleasant change to fix a meal for someone other than just herself.

She was fairly certain he wasn't much of a reader. He'd been rather reluctant to take the

KAY CORRELL

book she suggested. But she was sure if he just gave it a chance, he'd enjoy it. Sometimes people just needed to be reminded of how enjoyable it was to read. At least it was to her. She loved getting lost in a book. See how an author poked and prodded a character and made them grow and change. She even loved to see how a mean character or villain developed.

She read a bit of everything. Thrillers, women's fiction, romance—spicy or sweet—and legal thrillers. A bit of paranormal. Cozy mysteries. To be honest, she rarely met a type of book she didn't enjoy at least trying.

Romance books these days sometimes annoyed her though. So many focused on finding love in your twenties or thirties. How about older people? Didn't they deserve love, too? Not that she was looking for a relationship. She loved her life, and it was fulfilling and brought her much joy.

She wasn't sure she'd add anything to the mix... like a man. Besides, what did she know about relationships? The last serious relationship she'd had was years ago and had pushed her on her quest to find a new place to live. So even though the relationship had ended terribly, it had been the thing that brought her to Moonbeam all those years ago. And the pain had lessened over the years. She rarely thought about… *him*… anymore.

Enough of that.

She took one last look around the kitchen and headed downstairs. She'd head to church, then come back and open the shop at noon. Her regular Sunday routine.

Promptly at noon, she was flipping the sign on the shop to open. A steady stream of customers filled the shop all afternoon. The Leonards came in with their two little girls, and each girl picked out a book with their birthday money clutched in their hands, arguing about who found the best book. Emily popped in to rave about the history book she'd gotten and how great it was, then swept out in a whirlwind of energy.

Late afternoon, the Jenkins twins came in, their eyes sparkling with excitement. "Oh, Collette. Guess what?" Jillian said as they hurried up to her.

At least Collette was pretty sure it was Jillian. "What?"

"We found out what's going into the new

shop on Magnolia near Parker's General Store. It's going to be a flower shop. Isn't that exciting? We won't have to go to Belle Island anymore for flowers."

"I hadn't heard that." It would be nice to have a flower shop nearby. She wouldn't mind picking up flowers to place around the shop regularly. That was one thing she didn't like about living above the shop. No place for a garden. But it was a fair tradeoff for her easy commute to work… just down a flight of stairs. Plus, she loved her view up above Magnolia Avenue. A lovely place to people watch or just sit in the window seat and read.

"Yes, some lady named… What was her name, Jackie?" Jillian frowned.

"Her name was Daisy. How could you forget? Daisy as an owner of a flower shop. How appropriate." Jackie rubbed her hands in delight. "It's just perfect."

"And I heard she bought a little cottage on the beach. Near Blue Heron Cottages. But isn't it unusual that a stranger would just move to town and open a flower shop? I wonder why she chose Moonbeam?" Jillian's brow creased. "I hope we get a chance to meet her soon."

"And we can ask why she chose Moonbeam." Jackie bobbed her head.

Collette smiled at the pair. Always wanting to be the first to know anything and everything that was happening around town. "I guess we'll find out soon enough."

"We should. I hear the store is opening soon," Jillian said and turned to Jackie. "We should go. I want to stop by Parker's and see if Donna has heard about the flower shop opening."

They headed out the door. Obviously, they hadn't stopped in to buy a book, just to share their newfound information. She smiled as they left. They were quite a pair, bustling around town spreading news… and sometimes gossip. One thing was for sure, if you wanted something kept a secret, you didn't let the twins know.

The day passed in a steady stream of customers. Rose still hadn't dropped by to pick up her book, so Collette decided to drop it by the cottages after work. Besides, a nice walk sounded like a perfect way to end her day.

At five o'clock—she closed early on Sundays —she flipped the sign to closed and headed out toward the cottages, tucking the book under her arm.

The rain last night had scrubbed the town clean. The sun slanted through the sky, unlike last night when a cloud cloak had covered it. Rays of light filtered through the palm fronds and made dancing patterns on the sidewalks.

She made her way to the cottages and entered the open door to the office. Violet looked up from the reception desk. "Collette, hi. What brings you here?"

She held up the book. "I decided to deliver Rose's book. Besides, it's a nice evening for a walk."

"It is, isn't it? It cooled off nicely after last night's rain. Do you want me to hold the book for her? She comes by every morning for coffee. Or you could bring it to her cottage. I'd deliver it for you, but I'm the only one here at the desk right now. She's in the last cottage. The peach one."

"I'll drop it off to her."

"Hey, did the Jenkins twins stop by the shop and tell you the big news?"

Collette laughed. "They did. And they were headed to Parker's after the bookshop."

"They made it by here, too. Exciting news. A florist. It will be nice for when people have weddings here at the cottages though. They'll be able to get the flowers locally."

"That will be nice."

A couple came in and Violet greeted them. Collette turned to leave. "Catch you later."

She walked through the courtyard, passed the cottage she'd seen Mark come from at happy hour, and wondered what he was up to and if he'd explored any more of the town. Not that it was any of her business. She just wanted him to feel welcome was all.

She found the last cottage, and Rose was sitting on the porch, sipping a tall glass of lemonade. "Rose, special delivery." She held up the book.

"Oh, Collette. How nice. But you didn't have to bring it over. I started there yesterday, but then the storm threatened and I decided to postpone. Then today I got caught up in my knitting. Violet has been so nice to me. I wanted to knit something for her. Not a lot of need for knitting down here like sweaters or socks, but I decided to knit her some nice placemats and cotton dishcloths. Just to let her know how much

I appreciate her kindness."

Collette sat down in the chair next to Rose. "Oh, that placemat is so pretty. I love how the colors change in it. Nice and bright. Violet will love it."

"I hope so." Rose stood. "Let me grab another glass. Join me for lemonade?"

"I'd love that."

Rose returned, poured another glass, and sat back down. "I've just been sitting out here enjoying the view while it's still light enough to knit." She picked up her needles.

Collette sipped the lemonade, looking out at the peaceful view of the water with the waves rolling to shore. Occasionally she thought of buying a place on the water—she did love a good beach walk—but then she realized how practical it was to live above the shop. Plus, she'd redone the kitchen a few years ago with new appliances and cabinets. And new lighting, so the kitchen was nice and bright. Her bedroom in the back was large and spacious, and she'd redone the old bathroom with updated cabinets and a large walk-in shower. She'd hate to leave it now that she had it just the way she liked it.

The gentle clicking of Rose's knitting needles floated through the air. A bird called above them as it chased another gull. Peace settled over her. She glanced over at Rose's knitting. "I admire people who do handiwork like that knitting. I don't do anything like that."

"I find it very relaxing."

"I spend most of my free time reading." She smiled at Rose. "Occupational hazard, I guess. But I do love my books."

"As long as you're taking time out for yourself, that's what's important. Too many people just rush through their days. Never relaxing. Never taking time to just sit." Rose leaned back in her chair. "These days I'm quite the sitter. I go out and catch the sunrise, breathe the fresh salt air. Just… exist in the moment."

"I should do that more. Jody keeps nagging me to take more time off."

"You should." Rose glanced over at her. "We get one shot at our life. We should try and enjoy all the moments. The big ones. The small ones. The extraordinary, ordinary moments."

Rose was a wise woman. Collette smiled at her. "You're right. That's good advice. And I'll take it to heart."

CHAPTER 6

M ark spent Sunday alternating between listening to the book and researching on his laptop. He searched for classic books he was fairly certain Collette had read, and *Pride and Prejudice* had come up first. He clicked on a summary of the book and had the computer read it out loud to him. He checked that one off but wasn't really into it. Then he moved on to *The Great Gatsby* and then *Jane Eyre*. None of these were his type of book, and thank goodness the summaries weren't too long, but he thought he should at least know about some classics. He could drop a comment in conversation with Collette. Make it look like he actually knew something about books.

After his research, adding in Wuthering Heights—hey, Emily Brontë and Charlotte Brontë were *sisters*—he went back to listening to his book over a quick peanut butter sandwich. He finally stood and paced the room, waiting for the chapter to end. He would force himself to stop listening at the end of this chapter. Really, he would. But then, he'd said that about the last two chapters. How did people who loved to read get anything done?

He walked outside and sank onto a porch chair, closing his eyes and listening to the story. Who knew he could get this engrossed in a book? And why hadn't he tried audiobooks before? Violet's brother, Rob, was a really good author. If he saw him, he'd tell him what a great writer he was. And coming from him, that was quite a compliment, because he'd never thought a writer was great before.

He sensed someone standing before him and looked up, startled, to see Collette standing there. He yanked his headphones out of his ears. "Oh, hi."

"Hi. I was just visiting with Rose and saw you out here. Didn't mean to interrupt your listening."

"No, that's fine. I was just…" No, he wouldn't admit he was listening to the book. He set down his phone, detached the headphones, and wrapped the cord up neatly. "I'm not busy. I was just thinking of going to get something to eat."

"Oh, I won't keep you then," Collette said.

"No, that's fine. I'm in no hurry. Would you like a beer? I'm afraid that's all I have to offer."

She laughed. "I just had a lemonade with Rose, but a beer sounds great. I'll join you."

He disappeared inside, grabbed two beers, popped off their caps, and started to head back out. Oh, wait. She'd probably want a glass. He grabbed one and headed outside.

She reached for the offered beer. "No, the bottle is fine. I don't need a glass."

He stepped inside and set the glass on the table, then dropped back into his seat. He reached to move his phone, and the audiobook started to play again, blaring out the voice of the narrator. Fumbling with the phone, he tried to turn it off and dropped it. The narrator rambled on. He sent a furtive look toward Collette as he struggled to silence it.

She leaned forward, looking at him intently. "Are you listening to Rob's book?"

He closed his eyes for a moment, embarrassed to be caught. "I… I am. I'm not much of a reader, I'm afraid."

"You could have told me that."

He could have. And then she would have thought he was dumb. Just like his mother had always told him. Too dumb to read. Too dumb to learn anything. "I just—" He shrugged, unwilling or unable to explain it to her, wrapped up in his embarrassment.

"That's okay. But you should let me take back the paperback. Are you enjoying the story?"

"I am. It's really great. I've hardly gotten anything done all day. I keep saying just one more chapter."

She laughed. "I'm always saying that to myself. Often late at night when I really should be sleeping. And I'm glad you're enjoying it."

"But you don't have to take the book back. It's fine."

"No, I practically forced it on you. I insist. And next time, I'll suggest an audiobook for you to listen to."

"If you can find me one as good as this one, I'm all for it." He nodded, surprised at himself. Who knew he could love a book this much?

"Did you know if you buy an e-book, you can have your phone read it to you? It's not all fancy like a narrator, but you can at least have it read."

"I guess I never thought of that." He took a breath. "I sometimes have my computer read things to me. It's just… easier." He glanced over, waiting for that look that he'd seen so often. The look that said someone thought he was stupid.

"That's a smart thing to do."

He didn't hear *that* often. That something he did was smart.

"Some people just don't like to read." She shook her head. "But then, there are things I don't like to do, either. Everyone has their likes and dislikes."

She was so easy to talk to that he almost told her. Almost. But he just couldn't get the words out. It had been drilled into him for years to keep it a secret. His mother said people would call him a dummy. And quite often in school, they had.

"You know, my best friend growing up didn't

like to read. She was one of the smartest people I've ever met but hated reading. It wasn't until high school we found out she was dyslexic. Back then, they didn't have as many resources and coping skills taught like they do now. I often wonder if she ever found a way to deal with it all. But I moved away and I've never been back. Haven't spoken to her since then. Everyone wasn't all over social media like they are now."

This would be the time to speak up... and yet, he couldn't quite do it. Too many years of hiding it. He could hear his mother's voice playing over and over in his mind. *Don't tell people. They'll find out how dumb you are.*

"Anyway, here I am, rambling on. You get me talking about reading or books, and there's no stopping me." She reached for her beer and took a sip, her slim fingers wrapping around the bottle as she raised it to her lips.

He shouldn't be staring at her.

"I should let you go get your supper." She set the bottle down, and the pale pink color of her nail polish mesmerized him.

"No, wait." The words just blurted out of their own accord. "How about going to dinner with me? My treat." He paused. "You know, to pay you back for feeding me last night," he rushed on, not wanting her to think he was really asking her on a date or anything. That would be too forward. They'd just met.

"I'd love to go to dinner with you. I'm starving. Where would you like to go?"

"How about you pick?" Was he actually going to dinner with her? How did this happen?

"How about Jimmy's on the Wharf? Casual, great food, great view."

"Sure." He was willing to go with anything she suggested. And it wasn't like he knew the places around here.

"Do you want to walk? It's not too far."

He nodded. Maybe a nice stroll would take the edge off the surge of nervousness that now flowed through him.

CHAPTER 7

Collette couldn't remember the last time she had a date. Not that this was really a date. But it was a dinner out with a man. Okay, that was close to a date. Anyway, she enjoyed his company and had been pleasantly surprised by his offer.

And he didn't really know anyone in town. She hated for him to eat alone. It was mostly for that reason she'd said yes. At least that was the story she was trying to convince herself of.

She didn't know why this man fascinated her. His quiet demeanor. His friendly smile. The way he listened to her when she talked as if he was truly interested in everything she had to say.

She went down the steps with Mark right

beside her. They walked through the courtyard and out onto the sidewalk. "It's this way." She pointed. "Not far. It's on the bay."

They walked comfortably side by side, and she pointed out things as they strolled along, showing him the town. "That's where the Jenkins twins live, in that pretty old house. They grew up there and have lived there all their lives. They're kind of the town gossips, but good-hearted. They came by today to tell me the news of a new floral shop opening up in town. And that's the marina, just behind that row of buildings." She pointed as the tall masts of sailboats peeked above the buildings. They got to the marina with a mix of sailboats, large yachts, and well-loved, weathered fishing boats. After they passed it, she led him out onto the wharf.

Mark's eyes widened as they walked down the wharf. The crowd of people bustling by, the shops where customers trailed in and out, the lights strung across the walkway. He swung his gaze, taking it all in.

"This is quite the place," he said as they moved aside to let a family of four pass by.

"It is. You should see it at Christmas. We go

all out. A big tree with a tree lighting ceremony. Lots of lights. Each store decorates their windows. It's kind of magical."

"Sounds like it. Summerville doesn't do anything like that. Maybe a few decorations in the store windows. No tree lighting or anything. We do have the first graders at the elementary school make paper snowflakes for the hardware store—not that we'll ever see real snow—and sign them and we hang them around the store. The kids come in with their parents and hunt for the one they made. Brings in nice traffic to the store."

"That's a brilliant marketing idea. Was that your idea? I bet it does bring in all the families."

His face reddened. "Uh, yes. I thought of it. We've been doing it about ten years now. It's kind of a first-grader rite of passage in the town. The kids love it."

"That's great. Hm… wonder if I could do something like that." She shook her head, tucking away the thought, then turned to him, laughing. "But I thought it was some kind of requirement that all small towns had tree lighting ceremonies. Anyway, Moonbeam goes all out."

They continued strolling down the wharf, and she led him into Jimmy's as amazing aromas circled around them.

Aspen greeted her as they walked up to the hostess desk. "Collette, great to see you."

"Aspen, have you met Mark? He's staying at the cottages."

"No, I haven't." Aspen reached out and shook Mark's hand. "Nice to meet you."

"Aspen works at the cottages and lives there, too."

"But I've been busy here working at Jimmy's the last few days. We're short-staffed." Aspen grabbed two menus. "A table outside by the railing?"

"Please. I want to show off our sunsets." Collette followed Aspen through the restaurant and out onto the wide, open deck. They took their seats.

"I'll send your server right over." Aspen walked over toward the bar and stopped to chat with Walker Bodine for a moment, her face glowing with a wide smile.

"That's Aspen's boyfriend." She nodded toward the bar area. "Walker Bodine. His family owns Jimmy's. She works here and for Violet.

Violet said she didn't know what she did before Aspen started working for her at the cottages."

Mark glanced over toward the bar. "You seem to know everyone."

She laughed. "I guess I do. I've been here a long time."

He pored over the extensive menu, then finally looked up, bemused. "I give up. So many choices. What do you suggest?"

"I like the grouper. And I always get a side of slaw and hushpuppies."

Mark set his menu down. "That sounds good. I'll have that."

They ordered and sat talking as they sipped their drinks. "So, we're both in retail," Collette commented, wanting to know more about Mark. "Do you like it?"

"I guess so. It's all I've ever done. I do like taking care of the orders, setting up displays, figuring out sales we could have to bring in more business. Mr. Mason leaves most of that up to me these days. The hardware store has been in his family for a couple of generations. When I first started working there, his dad ran the place. When his dad retired, Mr. Mason was an only child, and it was always assumed he'd take over the store. I don't think his heart is really into it, though. He's a volunteer fireman, head of the school board, and just about every other thing you can think of in town. Pretty sure he's going to run for mayor this next election."

"So he leaves a lot of it up to you?"

"He does. And I enjoy it. We're running at a good profit these days."

"So that's why you don't take many days off? Because he depends on you? He should give you more time off."

"Oh, he gives it to me. I just don't take it." Mark shrugged.

"I'm glad you're taking this nice break now."

His eyes said he thought she was crazy and he'd rather be back at work. But then, they could both be cut from the same cloth. She rarely took time off, either.

Their meals came, and he dodged her next few questions, always changing the subject, so she decided to drop it. He obviously didn't want to talk about himself. They ate their meals and Mark insisted it was one of the best meals he'd ever had.

The sky put on a spectacular sunset, and

they sat after their dinner, finishing their drinks and watching the magical changing colors.

"You were right. Moonbeam does know how to throw a sunset," Mark said as the colors started fading and a few stars started to blink in the sky.

"We do." She nodded, pleased the sky had cooperated tonight after bragging on how Moonbeam did sunsets.

She offered to split the bill with him, but Mark insisted he had it. He paid, and they headed down the wharf. The crowd had thinned. Moonbeam was not a late-night town, by any means.

They stood at the end of the wharf. "I'm this way, and the cottages are that way." She pointed each direction.

"I'll walk you home," Mark said quickly.

"You don't have to do that. I walk around town at night by myself all the time. It's safe."

"But I'd like to. Give me a chance to stretch my legs."

She nodded. "Okay." They headed out to Magnolia Avenue.

As they walked, she chatted about the shops they passed and who owned them. He slowed down when sirens sounded in the distance. The sound got louder, and he paused. A fire truck and police car raced down the road.

He'd grown pale and leaned against the brick wall of the nearest shop. "You okay?" She reached out and touched his arm.

He jerked his arm away, his eyes darting, glancing up and down the street. "I'm... fine."

But he obviously wasn't.

The sirens faded as the vehicles disappeared into the distance. The color slowly came back to his cheeks. Still, he leaned against the storefront, taking obvious deep breaths. Finally, he pushed off the wall.

"You sure you're okay?" she asked quietly, not sure what had just happened to him.

He nodded, running his fingers through his hair.

They continued until they reached her shop, then went around back. She paused at the door. "Thank you for dinner."

"You're welcome." He still looked a bit shaky.

"So, what are your big plans for tomorrow?" she asked.

"I don't know. I'm hoping to finish the book, though."

"The bookshop is closed on Mondays, so I'm headed to Belle Island to the antique store there. I need another bookshelf."

"Of course you do." He laughed and relaxed a bit. Good.

"Would you like to come along? Belle Island is beautiful." She looked at him expectantly, not sure why she'd invited him along. Except for the fact he didn't know anyone else here thing. And everyone loved visiting Belle Island.

"Ah… yes. I'd like that."

"Great. How about you come by about ten tomorrow? We'll go to the island and then grab lunch at Magic Cafe. You'll love it. It's right on the beach."

"Sounds good. I'll see you tomorrow."

He turned and disappeared around the corner.

She slowly climbed the stairs to her apartment. By the time she got to the window and looked down, he was gone.

She wasn't sure what had happened to him when the fire truck and police raced past, but something had. She was sure of it.

CHAPTER 8

Violet made the coffee in the office the next morning, expecting Rose to come in any minute from her morning sunrise viewing.

Aspen came hurrying in. "Good morning."

"Morning," Violet said as she poured the water into the coffeemaker. "How was Jimmy's last night?"

"Busy. But Walker finally hired two new people. It should calm down there a bit now. Thanks for letting me work so many extra shifts there the last few days. I hope I didn't leave you stranded."

"No problem. I'm just grateful to have your help when I do." She walked to the desk. "Rob told me he's moving out to his own place."

"He is? Good for him."

She eyed Aspen. "What does that mean?"

"I just mean, he's a grown man. Needs his own place and some privacy."

"But I like having him here."

"I heard that," Rob said as he entered the reception area, carrying a box under his arm. "I knew it. You love having me here at your beck and call."

"Nah, you're actually a pain in the rear." She quickly deflected. "I'll be glad to have my space back."

"And yet I won't be here to cover the desk or fix things."

"Or be here to annoy me and tease me," she tossed back at him. But she was going to miss him. A lot.

"I'm moving today. The cottage is all ready." He stood there staring at her, watching her closely.

She put on a wide smile. "Great."

He came over and wrapped his arms around her. "Ah, sis. I'll miss you."

She hugged him, then stepped back, clearing her throat and blinking her eyes. She was not going to cry. "I'm sure you'll love having your own place."

"I will. But… I will miss you. You can call me if you need any help."

"Hey, you're just down the beach a bit. I'm sure you'll be back to give me your opinion on anything and everything."

He grinned at her. "I'm sure I will," he called over his shoulder as he walked out the door.

She took a deep breath and turned to Aspen. "He's a pain to have underfoot all the time."

Aspen just shook her head, a slight smile playing at the corners of her mouth. "Right."

Rose came in, greeting them both. "Good morning."

"Hey, Rose. Grab a cup of coffee." Violet nodded toward the coffee stand.

Rose poured a cup and walked up to the desk. "Got time to sit outside for a few minutes? It's lovely out this morning."

"Yes, we do. Come on, Aspen. Let's take five."

"Yes, Violet can tell you all about how she's

not going to miss Rob living here." Aspen rolled her eyes as she settled on her chair.

"I'm not going to miss him," Violet insisted.

Rose looked over at her with an indulgent, sympathetic look.

"Really, I'm fine." Violet took a sip of her coffee, avoiding Rose's glance.

"Oh, I met one of our guests last night at Jimmy's. Mark somebody. He was with Collette. Didn't catch his last name." Aspen changed the subject. Thank goodness.

"Mark Wheeler, sky-blue cottage," Violet said automatically.

"He seemed nice," Aspen said over the rim of her coffee mug.

"He is nice. He joined me out on the beach yesterday morning for sunrise." Rose leaned forward. "Though he has a bit of sadness around his eyes. Or something like that. Maybe a haunted look."

"I noticed that about him, too. I hope he relaxes during his stay and whatever is bothering him lessens while he's here." Violet looked out toward the water. "It's hard to stay upset when you have the sea to look at, isn't it?"

"I find the waves and the ocean very

comforting," Rose said, a faraway look in her eyes.

Speaking of sadness in their eyes. It hadn't escaped Violet that Rose had that look, too. But she'd never brought up the subject of her sadness in any of their conversations. Maybe when Rose was ready, she'd open up to her. Rose had just reserved her cottage for another month. She seemed in no hurry to leave. Which suited Violet just fine. She loved chatting with Rose and having her around. And it meant another cottage was rented for a whole month. That was nice, too. Especially during the slow season.

They chatted for about half an hour before Violet stood. "I should get back to work."

"Me, too." Aspen got up and headed inside.

"I'm going to start reading that book Collette dropped off for me last night. And I noticed she headed out with Mark last evening. From what Aspen said, they must have gone to dinner at Jimmy's together."

"Good for Collette. Evelyn said that Collette doesn't really date anyone. Just works at her bookshop all the time except for when she closes it for two weeks each year and heads out on one of her big adventures."

"People shouldn't work all the time." Rose eyed her.

"Hey, I hired Aspen to help me."

"And yet, you still work all the time." Rose smiled, climbed down the steps, and headed to her cottage.

Hey, she was working on it. Maybe she'd even take the afternoon off and go see Rob's new place. Maybe. But she really needed to weed the courtyard, and the lock on the yellow cottage was sticking—not that she knew anything about fixing locks. Rob did that kind of stuff for her. But she wasn't going to ask him. She wasn't.

Evelyn stood in the kitchen of Rob's cottage. It was a nice, cozy kitchen. Just enough room to not feel crowded, but not overwhelming or fancy. She unpacked a box of pots and pans that he'd had in storage. She quickly washed each one and set it on the drainboard.

His dishes were wrapped in bubble wrap,

and she couldn't decide if she should just put those on the shelf, or wash them, too.

Rob came into the kitchen and laughed. "They're fine. They were clean when they were put in the wrap. Just put them in the cabinet."

"You sure?" She frowned.

"I'm positive."

He took a dish from her hand and placed it up in the cabinet. "The movers just left. Not that I brought much with me. My stuff was dark and heavy in my home in Vermont. Didn't seem right for a beach cottage, so I sold most of it off and gave some away."

"We'll get you some furniture. A nice comfortable sofa. And a recliner. I know you like those."

"At least the last owner left the bookshelves. I brought a bunch of boxes of books. I can't quite seem to move to e-books. I like my paperbacks and hardcovers." He walked over to her and wrapped his arms around her. "I really like having my own place. We can have some privacy without Violet and her constant yammering."

She reached up and touched his face. "And yet, you'll miss her and worry about her."

He sighed. "I will. But we won't tell her that, now will we?"

She loved how close he was to his sister. And even if he complained about her scattered ways and her sudden decisions—like buying the resort when she'd never run one before—he still adored her. Teased her. Helped her out when she needed it.

She'd gotten closer to her own sister, Donna, the last year. Their whole family had gotten closer. She loved how strong the Parker women had grown. They had plans for brunch at Donna's house on Sunday. Just the women in the family. The guys were going to make a day of fishing. She loved being part of a big family. At least now that they were all close. She'd spent years avoiding them and regretted it now. Even her mother, after years of being standoffish and judgmental, had softened.

She leaned her face against Rob's chest, feeling his heartbeat. "There's something I wanted to talk to you about," he said softly as he tightened his arms around her.

"What?" she murmured into this chest.

He loosened his arms, and she looked up at him, his face serious.

"It's just… There's something I want you to know."

She waited. Patiently. Okay, not so patiently. What was this big thing he had to tell her?

He reached out and touched her chin, tilting her face up toward his. "I love you, Evelyn. You mean everything to me."

She stared up at him. "You… you love me?"

His lips curved into a soft smile. "I think I just said that. I'm so happy when I'm with you. You're fun, and comfortable to be with, and beautiful. And you bring me such joy. You're a best friend and lover, all wrapped into one."

She swallowed as her eyes filled with tears. "Oh, Rob. I love you, too. So much. I never knew I could be this happy."

He wrapped his arms around her again and pulled her close. "You, Evelyn Carlson, are the best thing that ever happened to me."

She leaned against him, feeling his warmth, feeling his love. Feeling safe and certain she was in the right place, here in his arms. She tilted up to look at him again and grinned. "Can you say it again?"

"I love you. To the moon and back, multiple times." He grinned. "So how about we take advantage of this privacy and celebrate our new declarations of love? Dinner here tonight?"

"Sounds wonderful. But first, we need to go to the market. You have no food at all here. We need staple items, plus anything else you want to get."

"You're the cook and baker. Whatever you say I need, we'll get. I'm more of a grab a peanut butter sandwich or a bowl of cereal kind of guy with an occasional steak grilled out."

She shook her head. "That's why I'm always sending over food from Sea Glass Cafe."

He patted his stomach. "And I appreciate it."

A powerful combination of peace mixed with excitement thrummed through her. Rob Bentley loved her. The childhood rhyme popped into her mind. *Rob and Evelyn sitting in a tree. K-I-S-S-I-N-G.* She laughed out loud.

"What?" He looked at her questioningly.

She just shook her head and smiled. "You don't want to know…"

CHAPTER 9

Collette was just coming downstairs when Mark got to the back door. She tugged it open and greeted him. "Good morning."

He answered with a wide smile. "Good morning to you. I'm all set for our expedition. Getting you another *much-needed* bookcase," he teased.

"I do need another one. And I have just the space. Okay, I moved furniture around to make more space. This one is going into my bedroom."

"Ah, wouldn't want to have to walk all the way into the main part of your apartment to get a book, now would we?"

"No, we wouldn't. Not that I don't have

three books sitting on my nightstand as we speak." She grinned and headed over to her minivan. With the back seat folded down and the middle seats folded forward, she should be able to fit the bookshelf in. If not, they'd tie it on the rack on the roof.

They drove to Belle Island and the large antique store, Bella's Vintage Shop. They headed inside and were greeted by Bella herself. "Good morning. Welcome to the shop. Can I help you find anything?"

"I'm looking for another bookshelf. Plus, anything else that catches my eye. I love your shop."

"Thank you." Bella's eyes sparkled with pleasure at the compliment. "The large furniture is in the back. I actually just got in three new bookshelves. Old ones, not new, of course. But new to the shop. One is a wonderful handmade one out of maple. Whoever made it carved their initials in the back and the year 1925."

"Oh, that's the year *The Great Gatsby* was published," Mark said, looking a bit surprised he'd blurted that out.

"Was it? I knew it was in the early 1920s."

She glanced over at him, surprised he knew a detail like that since he'd made it clear that he wasn't a reader.

They headed toward the back of the store, but not before she picked up a wooden bowl that caught her eye and a large glass vase that she wanted to fill with shells and put on the table in the corner of her apartment.

The bookshelf was perfect. The maple shone with the hand-rubbed finish, well-worn over the years. As they pulled one edge forward, she ran her finger over the etched initials on the back. "This is so lovely. It will be perfect. I love the history of it."

Bella helped them put the bookcase on top of the van and tie it down. "I'm glad it's going to someone who will appreciate it… not just paint it white or something." She laughed.

"No, that finish is too beautiful to be painted over."

They pulled away, and she drove down Oak Street, past the live oak and the gazebo at the end of the street. They headed over to Magic Cafe and she found a parking spot. Their footsteps crunched as they crossed the crushed shell drive and went inside.

"Collette, so nice to see you." Tally greeted them and gave her a big hug.

"I know. It's been a while." She turned toward Mark. "And this is Mark Wheeler. He's staying at Blue Heron Cottages and I brought him along for a little shopping expedition to Bella's shop, then promised to feed him lunch."

"You've come to the right place." Tally smiled, and they followed her through the building and out to the deck on the edge of the beach.

"You friends with Tally, too?" Mark asked as Tally left and they sat down.

"Yes, we got to be friends soon after I got to Moonbeam. I heard about Magic Cafe and came here one time when Tally was having a slow day. She saw me sitting alone and sat down and we talked for hours. Been friends ever since."

"You really do know everyone."

She laughed. "Not everyone. But a lot of people."

They ordered sweet tea, then perused the menus. "I love the grouper here. Though, the red snapper is good, too. I get the grouper fried. Delicious light batter."

"You talked me into it. I could get used to grouper for every meal." He set down his menu.

They ordered their lunches, and she took a sip of the cool tea. "Ah, this is good. Just a hint of sweet. Just like I like it." She set it down, and a drop of condensation rolled down the side of the glass and onto the pressed paper coaster emblazoned with Magic Cafe.

"This place has a great view. Look at that crystal clear water out there. Shades of emerald and teal." Mark stared out at the gulf.

"It is pretty, isn't it?"

"We don't have much that I would call a view in Summerville. A lot of parched land. Palm trees. We do have a small city park with one old live oak. You get more breezes than we do, too. Most of the year it's stifling muggy inland."

"I do love living right on the coast. When I was looking for a place to settle, I did browse around the East Coast some. The Outer Banks area, then the beaches near Charleston, then the St. Augustine area of Florida. But once I came to Moonbeam on the gulf, I knew I'd found where I wanted to stay."

"You lived in all those places?"

"For a bit. Couple months here and there."

"Wow. That's amazing. I've lived in the same town my whole life."

She guessed it was kind of amazing to someone who had only lived in one spot. She'd enjoyed it. But then had gotten tired of never feeling like she belonged. She'd longed to put down roots. And when she found Moonbeam and Beachside Bookshop, she found her home. "I do love it in Moonbeam. I came there at nineteen and I've been there forty years."

It took a minute, but he did the math. She was nine years older than he was. That surprised him. And strangely, it bothered him a bit. It shouldn't, but it did. He could hear his mother's voice. *What would people think?*

Of course, he was always hearing her voice in his mind on every little subject. Even though she'd been gone for years, he could still hear her voice. Correcting. Criticizing.

He almost blurted out she didn't look that old but caught himself just in time. Afraid he'd say the wrong words. That it would come out wrong, not as the compliment he meant.

That was from his mother, too. She always said he was terrible at words. Always saying the wrong thing. Her litany of his shortcomings played over and over in his mind, even when he tried to drown them out.

As they ate their lunch, Collette went on to tell him about the vacations she took each year to so many places. Her eyes lit up as she talked excitedly about the different countries she'd been to. People she'd met there. Places she'd visited.

As she talked, he wondered why she'd even asked him to come along today. She couldn't possibly be interested in a guy like him. A non-reader. Not a world traveler like she was. He always had to use his phone to calculate a tip, and thank goodness for spellcheckers on the phone and computer. He bet she did math in her head. Quickly. Not stumbling through it like he'd just done to figure out her age.

He'd probably bore her to tears if she got to know the real him.

Her talk turned to books, as it often did. Here

was his chance. He threw out a comment about *The Great Gatsby* since he'd brought it up earlier today. See, it paid to memorize little details. Like the year the book had been published.

"It was a fascinating book, with lots of symbolism," Collette said.

Symbolism? Had he read about symbolism? He'd thought it was just some poor schmuck yearning after a woman he couldn't have. And a tragic ending for lots of the characters. He racked his mind, trying to remember if he'd read about symbolism in the book. And why do people ruin a perfectly good story with talk of symbolism and theme and stuff like that?

The server came by to clear their plates with perfect timing. Because he had no idea about the symbolism. Looked like he needed to do another internet search. They split the bill this time, and he painstakingly did the math in his head, hoping he was right.

They headed back to Moonbeam, and she insisted on dropping him off at the cottages. He got out of her car and waved as she pulled away. Then he climbed the steps to his cottage, feeling dejected. He was not in her league. Not as smart as she was. She was pretty and funny and had tons of friends.

They hadn't made any plans to meet up again, which was good. He was afraid his inferiority complex would swallow him whole if he saw her again. He'd find a way to avoid her for the next two weeks. That's what he'd do. Then she'd never find out the truth about him.

A plan. He loved plans. They kept his life organized and predictable.

CHAPTER 10

Collette closed the shop the next evening and her stomach growled. She hadn't gotten to the market, and she was starving. Perfect excuse to walk over to Sea Glass Cafe and grab dinner.

She entered the cafe, and Melody called out. "Just grab a seat anywhere. Be with you in a minute."

She took a seat at a table by the window. She did like to people watch when she dined alone, which was most of the time. Oh, she occasionally went out with friends, but usually, it was just grabbing something to eat alone when she was too tired to face making a meal.

Melody came over and plopped a menu on

the table. "Evelyn is in the back and just pulled out another pecan pie. Make sure you save room for it."

"Oh, that sounds wonderful. I will save room."

Melody turned and waved to Ethan Chambers who was just coming in the door. "Hey, Ethan. Be with you in a sec."

"I'll just grab a seat at the fountain counter." He walked past them, smiled at Melody, and slipped onto a counter stool.

Collette could swear he blushed as he passed them by. Hm… She always thought that Ethan was a nice young man. And Melody was a recent widow. Well really, not so recent anymore. It had been a while.

But Melody seemed oblivious to any of the looks Ethan kept throwing at her. Ah, well. These things take time.

The door opened again, and Mark stood in the doorway, looking uncertain. Before she could think or stop herself, she waved. "Mark, come join me. I just sat down."

Was that reluctance on his face? If it was, it was quickly covered up by an easy smile. He walked over to the table. "You sure?" He nodded at the book she'd placed on the table. "Don't want to interrupt your reading."

"I'm sure. Sit." She motioned to the seat across from her. "Did you meet Melody at Violet's happy hour?"

"Yes, hi, Melody."

"Glad you came in," Melody said. "Let me go grab you a menu."

Mark settled into the chair across from her. "Uh… thanks for the invite."

He looked strangely uncomfortable, so she gave him her best welcoming smile. "Looks like we're having a lot of our meals together these days."

"Uh-huh." He took the menu Melody handed him.

"Can I get you guys some drinks?"

"Tea for me," Collette said.

"Same."

"We have Evelyn's meatloaf tonight. So good. Oh, and Mark, I was just telling Collette to save room for pecan pie. Fresh out of the oven. I'll be back with your drinks." Melody walked away, stopped to chat with Ethan for a moment, then disappeared into the kitchen.

"So, what did you do with your day?" Collette glanced at him from over her menu.

"I caught the sunrise this morning. Sat out with Rose."

"Ah, yes. Rose loves her sunrises, doesn't she?"

"After that, I finished the audiobook. It was so good. I downloaded the new book by that Gabe Smith that you recommended. Didn't get it started yet. Plan on starting it tonight."

"Did you like Rob's book?"

"I did. Did not really see the ending coming."

She looked up. "Speaking of Rob." She waved as he entered the cafe. "Rob, over here. Come meet your newest fan."

He came over and stood by the side of the table.

"Rob, this is Mark. He just finished your new book. Mark, this is Rob."

Mark stretched out his hand. "Rob, nice to meet you. I thoroughly enjoyed your book. Really liked it. I have no idea how you can think up a story like that."

"Thanks. Love to hear when readers enjoy my books."

"I did. Listened to it on audio."

"Oh, didn't my narrator do a good job? Well, I thought he did."

"He was great."

"So, Mark is staying at Violet's cottages," Collette said. "But I heard you moved out into your own place."

"No secrets in Moonbeam. I did move into my own place. Felt a bit like I was deserting Vi, but it was time."

"She's one of the most independent women I've ever met. She'll do fine."

"I'm sure she will. I just need to drop by and see what I can help her with. And don't tell her, but I miss getting up and seeing her. Even if she's impossibly messy and never puts anything where it belongs."

She smiled. "I'm sure Violet misses you, too."

"You'd never know it by how she was so enthusiastic about my moving out. She'd never tell me if she missed me, either. But I'm sure she does." Rob winked. "I'm going to duck into the kitchen and see Evelyn. Nice meeting you, Mark." He turned and disappeared into the kitchen.

"Rob and Violet are really close, no matter how much they tease each other or act like they don't need each other. They do. It's nice to see grown siblings so close." She shrugged. "Though I don't have any brothers or sisters. Do you?"

"Yes. An older brother, Miles."

Mark stifled a sigh. A perfect older brother. Smart. Captain of the high school baseball team. Took them to state... and they won, of course. Went to college on a scholarship. Now he was a hotshot investor and lived in California. Or at least that's where he lived the last time he'd heard. Mark had seen him exactly once since Miles had graduated from college. At their mother's funeral.

"Do you see him often?" Collette asked.

"Ah, no. Not in years." Fifteen years. And the sad thing was, he wasn't sure he even minded. He'd spent his youth being compared to his brother. Held up to his standards. Always hearing "why can't you be more like Miles?" And Miles had always made it clear that Mark was an embarrassment as a brother. In a way, it was easier to have his family all gone now, no longer chanting their lists of his shortcomings.

"That's too bad. I always imagined what it would be like to have a brother or a sister. I love reading about families in books. Seeing how close siblings can be."

"Well, not all siblings are like that." The words came out harsher than he meant. But was she criticizing him for not being close to Miles? An awkward silence settled between them.

She looked at him for a few moments and frowned. "Oh, I know. It just seems like some kind of magical fantasy to me. To have a sibling like that. I always wished for a sister. Or maybe an older brother. But I'm just being silly." She shook her head, and her hair bobbed on her shoulders. She reached for her tea and he was once again entranced by her slender fingers and pale pink nail polish. A small silver bracelet encircled her slim right wrist.

He pulled his gaze from her hands. He'd be glad to give her Miles for a sibling if she wanted one. Though, he wouldn't really wish Miles on her. He was cold, cutting, and ruthless.

Melody came to take their order, thankfully

interrupting the whole sibling discussion. They ordered their meals, both choosing the meatloaf, followed by slices of the most delicious pecan pie he'd ever had. Their conversation stumbled from one topic to silence to another topic and more edgy silence.

As they were finishing up, two women came into the cafe and hurried over to the table. "Oh, Collette. There you are. We saw you through the window."

"Here I am," Collette said. "Mark, this is Jackie Jenkins." She pointed to one woman. "And this is Jillian."

He stared at them both for a moment, like he was seeing double. Identical twins dressed in identical outfits. He remembered his manners and quit staring. "Nice to meet you."

"Mark is staying at Blue Heron Cottages."

"Oh, hasn't Violet done such a wonderful job with the resort? You should have seen it before. Murphy had just let that place get so run down." The one he thought was Jillian shook her head, a firm frown etched on her face.

"It was very sad. Very. We're so glad that Violet spruced it all up. We don't want anyone thinking that Moonbeam is a dying small town," the other twin chimed in.

"So you two? You know each other? You're dating?" Jillian—maybe—asked. Did he have them straight?

"Oh, no. I just met Collette at Violet's and came in here to eat. She was eating alone, so she asked me to join her."

"Being friendly," Collette added, almost too quickly.

"Hm... I thought we heard you two were at Jimmy's the other night. Together." Jackie looked at him, then at Collette, a knowing look in her eyes.

"We... were." Collette looked over at him and gave the slightest shrug of her shoulder.

"I see," Jillian said, a doubtful look in her eyes like they were trying to hide something. "Well, we found out more news about who is opening the flower shop. A single woman. Moving here all alone. She used to own a flower shop in Colorado. Colorado is a long way from Florida."

"I do so wonder why she chose Moonbeam." Jackie frowned.

The Jenkins twins. Now he remembered

Collette pointing out their house. The town gossips.

"Well, we should run. Do let us know if you hear anything else about this mysterious woman moving to town." The women turned in unison and headed for the door.

"They are... interesting." He looked over at Collette and shook his head.

"They are. Always wanting to spread the news. They'll probably spread it all over town that we're dating." She gave him a rueful smile. "Sorry about that."

He knew all about small-town gossip and had no desire to be the subject of it. He pushed back his chair. "I should go. I have a new audiobook calling to me." Being labeled as Collette's date was the last thing he needed. Hadn't he just last night made a plan not to see her anymore? How had that worked out for him? With all the restaurants in this town, he'd walked into the one where she was having dinner.

"Well, I never keep a person from their book." Collette rose and followed him outside. "Thanks for joining me for dinner. It was nice not eating alone for a change."

"Uh, sure." Now he felt like a jerk for trying to hide from her. She was just looking for some company so she didn't have to eat alone. That was all she wanted from him. He wasn't someone she'd be *interested* in.

"I guess I'll see you around?" Collette looked at him as if she were expecting… something?

He held his resolve. "Yes, probably." He turned and headed down the street in the opposite direction of her apartment, not realizing until a few minutes later that he was headed in the wrong direction. At least she hadn't called out and corrected him. Pointed out his stupid mistake. He took a side street, then turned around and headed back to the cottages, weaving in and out of the light from the streetlamps, suddenly feeling all alone. Which was totally not like him. He was always alone at night. And it didn't ever bother him. Not a bit. His life was just fine the way it was. Well, pretty fine.

There was *one* thing he wished he could change. But he couldn't change what happened, so there was no use wasting time with what-ifs.

The cottages came into view and gratitude

flowed through him when he didn't see anyone sitting out on the porch by the office. He wasn't in the mood for small talk. He hurried across the courtyard and entered his cottage.

The silence inside thundered around him. He flicked on a light, trying to chase away his thoughts. But the low glow from the lamp did little to lift his spirits.

Don't be an idiot, Mark. A smart woman like that would never be interested in you.

Maybe he should just call his boss tomorrow and see if he could head back home.

CHAPTER 11

E velyn finished cleaning up the kitchen at Sea Glass Cafe as Rob sat eating a piece of pecan pie. She loved it when he dropped by and kept her company while she finished up at the cafe.

She peeked her head out of the kitchen to make sure all the tables were clear. Melody and Ethan sat chatting at the ice cream counter. She closed the door and left them alone.

"It's all cleared up except for Ethan's malt glass. But he and Melody are chatting, so I just left them alone."

Rob looked up from his pie. "She should ask Ethan out."

"I don't think that's ever occurred to her."

"It doesn't look like old Ethan is going to get the nerve up very soon to ask her out. He just watches her with that lovesick expression on his face. How can she not see that?"

"I don't know. It's clear to everyone else. But I guess she just needs time. And I don't think she's over losing John. I'm sure it's hard to be a widow ever, but especially at such a young age."

Melody came into the kitchen, carrying the malt glass. "This is all that's left."

"Here, I'll take it." Evelyn reached for it.

"No, I've got it. You go ahead and leave. I'll get this, then lock up. Ethan said he'd walk me home. Said it's really nice out tonight."

Evelyn glanced at Rob and smiled. "Oh, well, have a nice walk." She hung up her apron. "You ready to go, Rob?"

"I am. Need to walk off that piece of pecan pie."

"You mean those two pieces of pecan pie?" She laughed. She loved that Rob enjoyed her cooking so much. Always bragging on her. Always telling her what a great cook she was, how pretty she was, and how much he enjoyed spending time with her.

It was such a change from all the years she

spent married to Darren. Darren never liked anything she did, anything she wore, anything she said. Always correcting her. Regularly cheating on her. She just didn't know why she stayed with him as long as she had.

But Rob was different. Kind. Caring. And she adored him. She looked up at him as they walked outside.

"What?" he asked.

She touched his face. "Nothing. I'm just… happy."

He kissed her lightly on the lips. "And I'm incredibly happy being with you."

He took her hand in his and they walked down the sidewalk, their steps in sync, her heart overflowing with love for this man.

Collette climbed the stairs to her apartment and flicked on the light switch. Mark seemed different tonight. A bit standoffish. Not like he was before. Maybe he'd been looking forward to a quiet meal by himself. She'd jumped in and butted into his life the last few days. Maybe he just wanted alone time. She resolved to not ask him to eat with her or do anything with her when she ran into him again.

Because surely she would run into him again, wouldn't she? It was a small town. And the thought of never seeing him again bothered her. But why? He'd only been here in town a few days. She hardly knew him.

And yet she felt like she *did* know him, even if she was certain he was hiding some pain or secret. There was that bit of a haunted look in his eyes at times.

But usually, they talked and laughed. An easy camaraderie. Well, until tonight at dinner. That had been filled with awkwardness. She hated that. She usually had a way of making anyone feel comfortable. But she hadn't been able to break through to Mark tonight.

She fixed a cup of tea, then wandered over to the window, settling on the window seat. A few people walked along the sidewalks below, but mostly it was quiet. Evelyn and Rob walked by, holding hands. She smiled as they paused under a streetlamp and Rob kissed Evelyn. Evelyn smiled, and they continued on. They were such a cute couple. She'd gotten to know Evelyn better this past year. Before that, Evelyn had run with the country club crowd, married to that pompous oaf, Darren. She was glad Evelyn had found someone who treated her well and obviously adored her.

Sometimes she wished she had that with someone. A friendship and more. Having someone you knew was always there for you. That you could depend on.

She'd had that once. Well, she'd *thought* she had that. She'd been so, so very wrong. But she learned her lesson and hadn't made *that* mistake again. She'd never let herself date someone who she wasn't positive exactly where she stood with them at all times. Which had limited her dating over the years, but that was okay. At least she'd never repeated her mistake.

And yet, sometimes it was lonely sitting up here in her window seat, watching the world go by outside. But she had a good life. A fulfilling one, even. She had her bookshop and her travels. Good friends. Her beloved apartment. Her books.

But occasionally, like tonight, she just wondered what more there could be.

CHAPTER 12

Violet looked up from the reception desk to see Rob walking in the door to the office. "You don't have to keep checking on me. I'm fine." She rolled her eyes.

"I know you are, but I thought I'd see if there's anything you need help with." He crossed over to the desk and leaned a hip against it.

"It's only been two days since you moved out." She shook her head but was secretly glad to see him. It had been strange getting up the last few mornings and not having him sitting at the breakfast table or joining her for coffee in the office.

She toyed with asking him to fix the lock on the yellow cottage. She'd been unsuccessful in her attempts to fix it and debated calling a locksmith.

He laughed. "I know there's something you want me to look at. I can tell by the look on your face."

She let out a long sigh. "Okay, okay. The lock on the yellow cottage keeps jamming."

"I'm on it." He grabbed the toolbox from under the reception desk—they needed it so often it was silly to put it away in the shed—and headed out.

Soon he returned and triumphantly swung the toolbox back under the desk. "All fixed."

Of course he figured it out when she couldn't. "Thanks." And she was thankful. It just annoyed her slightly that he could fix it in minutes when she'd spent an hour working on it with self-help videos pulled up on her phone, trying to follow the directions.

"I knew you'd miss me and my magic fix-it skills." He grinned smugly, holding his hands out in front of him, wiggling his fingers.

"I don't miss your know-it-all attitude." She glared at him.

"Maybe I *do* know it all," he teased.

"Ha." She turned her back on him.

"Are the cottages full?" He ignored her turned back.

"Pretty much." She kept her back turned and busied herself shuffling papers. Three were empty, but she wasn't telling him that. He'd just tell her she needed to advertise more. Get on social media. Et cetera, et cetera, et cetera. What did she know about social media? Exactly nothing.

He leaned against the reception desk, still ignoring her turned back. "So Evelyn and I had a kind of celebratory dinner the other night."

She whirled around and eyed him closely. "What kind of celebration?" And were his cheeks actually getting red?

"I… I told her how I feel about her." He looked down at his hand resting on the counter.

"You mean that you love her?"

"What?" His eyebrows shot up, his eyes full of surprise, then he grinned. "Yes, that. And she loves me, too."

"Of course you love her, you big goof. Anyone can see that. I can't believe it took both of you so long to figure it out."

"So maybe your brother is a slow study when it comes to women. But I eventually get things sorted out. I'm not very good at this dating and emotions things."

"No kidding," she said, only partly under her breath.

"Heard that. Anyway, I'm happy, sis. Evelyn is the kindest, most wonderful woman."

"Yeah, what does a woman like that see in you?" But really, her brother was quite the catch. Funny, handsome in an I-guess-he-is brotherly way, smart. Okay, he had too many opinions and didn't keep them to himself. Ever. But she did think that Evelyn and Rob were a good match. And she was happy for him.

Collette kept her promise not to ask Mark to do anything or eat with her for the whole day. It had been an easy promise to keep because she hadn't actually *seen* him all day. He didn't drop by the store and didn't show up when she decided to grab dinner at Sea Glass Cafe again.

That was good, right?

She sat at her table by the window, people watching—but *not* looking for Mark to walk by.

Melody came over with her dinner. "Here you go. One chicken salad sandwich on homemade bread and a fruit cup."

"Thanks." She reached for the plate.

"You eating alone tonight, huh?" Melody asked as she filled Collette's tea glass.

"Yes, just me." Didn't she usually eat alone when she was here? Just one tiny joint dinner with Mark and people expected her to have every meal with him? Okay, there was the dinner at Jimmy's and the lunch at Magic Cafe. But still.

Melody glanced around the cafe with only one other table of customers. "Mind if I join you for a bit? Would love to get off my feet."

"Sure. Sit."

Melody took the seat across from her. "So, are you going to go to Violet's happy hour again this Friday?"

"I don't think so. It's hard to get away from the shop then. I hate to ask Jody to work late on Friday, too. She's usually off at four."

"I bet she doesn't mind. She was in here the

other day telling me how much she loves working there. And she said she wished you'd take more time off. She thinks you work too hard."

She sighed. "Jody is always saying that. But I do take some time off."

Melody raised an eyebrow. "Really? When was the last time you took off a day except for Monday when you're closed?"

"Oh, it was…" She frowned. When was the last time she'd taken a day off? It wasn't last week. Or the week before. Was it sometime last month? Surely it wasn't that long ago.

"Ah, ha. Jody was right. You do work too hard."

"Look who's talking. It seems like you're either working here at the cafe or at Parker's store anytime I come in."

"Nope. Evelyn and Donna make sure I take two days off each week. The days vary, but I do take them off. It's nice to catch up on chores at home. Or sometimes I just go and take a long beach walk. Sometimes I just curl up on my front porch and read."

Maybe she really should take more time off.

Everything Melody just said she did on her days off appealed immensely to her. Maybe she'd take Sunday off this weekend. Maybe.

"So, do you have any more plans with Mark?"

"No, no plans. We just happened to run into each other last night and I asked him to join me."

"The Jenkins twins were in for lunch today and said you had dinner at Jimmy's with him earlier this week."

"Does the whole town think we're dating?"

Melody laughed. "Probably, if Jillian and Jackie think you are."

She shook her head. "I swear, they spread more gossip. No, I'm not dating him. Just being nice to a visitor to town." And yet, she was sorry she hadn't seen him today. Not that she'd admit it to Melody. She could barely admit it to herself.

Melody stood as a couple came into the cafe. "I better get back to work."

She sat and ate her dinner—alone. But that didn't bother her. She almost always ate alone. Only it had been fun and entertaining to eat meals with Mark. Talk to him. Hear about his life, what little he shared of it. Talk about her life and the bookshop and books.

Maybe he was tired of her yammering on about books all the time. Though, he had said he'd snagged another audiobook to listen to. Maybe she would turn him into a reader. Okay, an audiobook listener.

She finished her meal, paid Melody, and headed back to her apartment. The darkness and quiet of the apartment swirled around her. She crossed over to the window without flipping on a light and sat on the window ledge, watching the town below her.

A lone man came walking down the street, and she held her breath. Was it Mark? But as he got closer, she saw it was Delbert Hamilton. No Mark today.

This was silly. She'd only known Mark for six days—and the fact that she'd counted up the days annoyed her. Why was she looking for him? She probably would never see him again. And that was fine. It really was.

She had everything she needed in her life. But hadn't she sat up here in the same spot just last night trying to convince herself of that very same truth?

Did she have everything she needed? Everything she wanted?

She turned that thought over and over in her mind as she stared out into the night.

CHAPTER 13

Collette left work mid-afternoon on Thursday and let Jody close up. She was *almost* taking Melody's advice. It wasn't a full day off, but it was a few hours. That counted, right?

Feeling proud of herself, she decided to head to Sea Glass Cafe and indulge in a large vanilla shake. Or maybe a slice of pie with a scoop of ice cream. Either sounded like a great way to celebrate her time off.

She entered the cafe and wound her way back to the counter, slipping onto a stool. Melody came out from the back. "Hey, Collette."

"I took your advice. See? I left early.

Decided to reward myself with some ice cream."

"I kind of meant a whole day." Melody laughed as she moved behind the counter. "What can I get for you? We have fresh peach pie."

"Oh, that sounds good. A slice of pie with a scoop of vanilla ice cream."

Melody quickly fixed the dessert and slid it across the counter. "I have to admit, when I took a break earlier, I had a piece of that pie, too. So good."

She took a bite of the flaky, cinnamon-sweet pie with a bit of the ice cream. It really was a decadent delight, and she savored the taste. She plunged her fork in for another bite.

"Oh, look. There's Mark." Melody waved. "Hey, Mark. Come on over."

She swiveled slightly on the stool and saw him hesitate before slowly walking back to the counter. Why the hesitation? Was he avoiding her? The thought just popped into her mind, unbidden. Then it roared to the front of her mind.

"Mark." She nodded at him, *not* asking him to join her.

"Hey Collette, Melody. I ran into the Jenkins twins and they told me how great the ice cream was here and I thought I'd come try it."

"Take a seat. What would you like?"

He glanced above the counter at the list of all the delicious options. "I think I'll have a chocolate sundae."

"Good choice. We have the very best chocolate sauce ever and freshly made whipped cream." Melody busied herself with making the sundae.

Mark sat down beside her. She was adamant that this did *not* count as her asking him to join her. He came in of his own accord. Melody invited him over. This was not her fault. This did not break her promise to not invite him to do anything with her.

She stabbed the pie and took another bite as silence fell between them. He shifted on his seat, his knee bumping into her.

"Oh, sorry," he said quickly.

"No problem." She gently pried another tiny bite of the pie. Because suddenly, she wanted the treat to last a good long time. About as long as it took Mark to eat his sundae.

Melody slid the sundae over to Mark, along

with a long spoon. "Enjoy. I've got to run to the kitchen and load another stack of dishes. I'll be back out to check on you."

Mark took a bite of his sundae. She took a bite of her pie. She should talk to him. Ask him about his week. Something. How he liked the town. Wasn't the cooler weather nice? Was he enjoying the new book?

Instead, she took another bite of the pie, dismayed that it was almost gone. She quickly glanced at his sundae. He still had three-fourths of it left.

"I thought—"

"How was—"

They both laughed. "You first," she said with a nod.

Rob and Evelyn strolled down the street toward Sea Glass Cafe. He'd convinced her to take a long lunch with him, but now she insisted on getting back to the cafe before the dinner rush.

She tucked her hand on his arm, and he closed his hand around hers, enjoying just walking along with her. Feeling like he belonged here in Moonbeam. Belonged with Evelyn. He hadn't felt like he truly belonged anywhere in a very long time. Like since he'd been a kid. And he was way past his kid days now.

In the few days he'd had his new cottage, Evelyn had started transforming it into a home. Flowers in vases. Pictures on the walls. They'd found a nice wooden table at a thrift shop and put that in the kitchen. He'd found the perfect old desk that he put in the spare room he planned on making his office. Its window looked out over the water. He'd get some bookshelves soon. It would be the perfect spot to sit and write. She seemed to know all the places to shop. And Evelyn insisted they'd get more furniture for the family room—they'd found a sofa and a coffee table—as soon as they had more time.

He enjoyed making the cottage his home with Evelyn's help. Though, he still worried about leaving Violet. Maybe he'd stop by Blue Heron Cottages after he dropped off Evelyn. Just check in on her and see if she needed any help with anything. Though, she'd probably insist that she didn't, even if she did. She was stubborn like that.

"Are you working late tonight?" he asked.

"Yes, I'm closing. Emily is working, too. But I'm sending Melody home after the rush."

"I'll come by about nine to walk you home?"

She smiled up at him with a look that charmed him. "That would be nice."

He'd gotten used to walking her home at night. Their quiet time together. Smiles like the one she just gave him. Talking about their days. If he had his way, he'd spend all his free time with her. That thought shouldn't startle him, but it kind of did. Spend all his time with her...

"Hey, you know what?" He grinned.

She slowed and looked up. "No, what?"

"I kind of love you."

"I've heard a rumor to that effect." Her lips curved up in a gentle smile. "I kind of love you, too. Like a lot of kind of."

Happiness and contentment surged through him. He was right where he belonged. With Evelyn. By her side.

As they got to the corner across from the cafe, Evelyn let go of his arm and stepped off the sidewalk.

"Yoo-hoo! Evelyn. Rob."

He stopped and turned to see the Jenkins

twins hurrying toward them. He paused and waved, then swiveled back to tell Evelyn to wait a second as she stepped into the street. As he glanced back, he paused in horror as a green sedan sped toward her. "Evelyn!" He sprang forward, reaching, grasping.

The screech of tires.

Screams.

A thud more frightening than any sound he'd ever heard.

He lunged forward and dropped to his knees. Evelyn lay crumpled in the street as he knelt beside her. Voices surrounded him. Talking. Blending together.

"I'm sorry. I didn't see her."

"Is she okay?"

"Is that Evelyn?"

"She came out of nowhere."

But he could only focus on Evelyn. "I'm here. You're going to be okay." He murmured and touched her head. His hand came back with blood on it.

She moaned and opened her eyes, only to shut them quickly.

"Evelyn?" She didn't move. He reached for her wrist to feel her pulse.

More commotion around him, but he ignored it. He heard sirens in the distance. "Evelyn, stay with me. Help is coming. You're going to be okay. I promise." His heart pounded in his chest and he struggled to catch his breath. Would she be okay?

She had to be okay. There was no choice in it. He couldn't lose her.

"Evelyn?" Was her pulse slowing? His voice rose and he could hear the terror in it. "Evelyn!"

CHAPTER 14

M ark plunged his spoon into the tall ice cream dish. "Okay, I'll go first. I thought Gabe Smith's book was excellent." He took another bite of the sundae.

"Oh, you finished it?" Collette looked at him.

"It's about all I did yesterday and earlier today. Listen to the book. I even took a long beach walk while I listened to it. I couldn't stop."

She smiled at him. "I'm so glad you enjoyed it."

"But now you're going to have to suggest another one."

"You know me, I always have another book

suggestion."

He did know that about her. He actually
knew quite a bit about her after only a few days.
And he'd missed her yesterday, which was a bit
silly. And he'd looked up symbolism in The
Great Gatsby, too. Just in case she brought it up
again. Not that he had really planned on seeing
her again. But it appeared that fate had other
plans.

Suddenly, he paused, straining to hear a
sound in the distance. He froze in his seat,
dreading what he was sure he was hearing. Yes,
it was. Sirens. He gripped the edge of the
counter, no longer hearing whatever Collette
was saying to him. *Deep breaths, Mark. Deep
breaths.*

The sirens got louder and louder. Closer and
closer. His pulse roared through his veins,
pounded in his ears. The room spun around
him as if he were spinning the stool in crazy
circles, around and around. He closed his eyes,
but it didn't help.

"Mark?"

He could hear Collette's voice, but it
sounded like it was in the distance, not right
here next to him. Still, he didn't open his eyes.

He willed the sound to go away. His brother's taunting voice rang in his ears. *You're such a baby. Afraid of everything.*

"Mark." Louder this time, and he felt her hand on his arm. A touch on his cheek.

His jaw clenched, and beads of sweat gathered on his forehead. The sirens were right outside the cafe, deafening. Then, just as deafening, the sound of silence descended when the sirens shut off. He slowly pried open his eyes but could see flashing lights swirling around the cafe.

His heart pounded in his chest, and he took a few steadying breaths. Collette stood at his side, her arm around him. "Are you okay? No, you aren't. No matter what you say. You're not okay."

He turned and looked at her. "I'm…" He started to say he was fine. But he wasn't. And she knew it. He couldn't lie to her. "I'll be okay. Just give me a minute."

"I'll give you all the time you need, but then you need to talk to me. Please."

Melody hurried out from the kitchen, wiping her hands on a towel she was carrying. "Was that sirens I heard? Did they stop outside?"

"Yes, they're right outside the cafe," Collette said, still keeping her eyes locked on him.

Jillian and Jackie Jenkins dashed into the cafe, out of breath. "Oh, the most horrible thing happened." Jillian bent over, gasping.

"Yes, horrible." Jackie patted her sister's back, then turned to them. "Evelyn was hit by a car."

"Oh, no." Melody dropped the towel as the color drained out of her face. She rushed past the twins and fled out the door.

But Collette stayed firmly by his side, her arm around him, never wavering. He wasn't sure why she cared, why she stayed here with him, but he had to admit he was grateful for the support. He couldn't remember when someone had been there for him when he needed them. Certainly not his mother. Not his brother.

But here was Collette, by his side, wanting to help him.

Collette wanted nothing more than to walk Mark back to his cottage. Make sure he was okay... though his color was back, and he seemed fine now. He would argue with her, but she planned on winning this argument.

Melody came back into the cafe after the ambulance left. "Oh, poor Evelyn. I'm so worried about her. She looked so pale and there was so much blood. She slipped in and out of consciousness."

She wanted to say she was sure Evelyn would be okay, but she didn't really know if she would or not.

Melody stood and stared around the cafe. "I guess I'm on my own tonight. Evelyn is obviously not here. Emily rushed off with her mother to go to the hospital."

"I'll help." The words came out before she remembered she was going to take care of Mark.

"Really? That would be wonderful."

"I used to wait tables. Okay, it was a billion years ago, but I'll manage." She eyed Mark. "You could stay and have dinner."

"I think I'll just head back to my cottage." His glance darted toward the door as if he was planning his escape.

"Are you sure?" She still wasn't certain he should go anywhere on his own.

He nodded. "Sure, I'm fine. I promise." A look of relief swept over his face as if he were happy to avoid her questions. Maybe avoid *her*. There was that thought again. She still had questions. They would just have to wait until later.

He gave her a weak smile and hurried out the door at a pace that could *almost* be considered a run. Away from her. Pushing the thought aside, she turned to Melody. "Okay, where do you want me to start?"

They both turned at the sound of the door opening again. Ethan came rushing into the cafe. "I heard what happened. That's horrible. I hope Evelyn will be okay."

"Me, too." Melody leaned down and picked up the towel she'd dropped on the floor when she sped outside earlier. "I'm so worried."

"What she should be worried about is that I'm going to be her helper tonight for the dinner rush." She smiled, trying her best to cheer Melody up.

"I can help, too." Ethan insisted. "I know the menu. I can bus tables and run meals out. Do dishes. Whatever you need."

"I'm sure not going to turn down any help."

"Why don't you go on back into the kitchen and start the dinner prep? We can serve a limited menu tonight." She pushed Melody toward the kitchen. "It will be fine."

But would it? And she still felt guilty for letting Mark rush out of here. She would have felt better if he'd at least stayed for dinner so she could keep an eye on him. But the look on his face when he glimpsed an escape was crystal clear. He was out of here and glad to avoid her questions.

She worked until the last customers were gone and the cafe cleaned up. She was a little rusty at the whole waitress thing, but everyone who came in was patient because they'd all heard about the accident. Finally, Ethan insisted he'd help with the rest and she should go.

Melody locked the door behind Collette when she left. She really wanted to check on Mark, but it was late. She couldn't just appear on his doorstep out of nowhere, could she? Besides, he might be asleep.

Or maybe not even answer her knock because he was avoiding her. And as much as she wanted to know what was wrong, wanted to know what had happened, was it really any of her business? Wasn't it his story to tell when he wanted to tell it? Besides, he'd practically run away from her earlier.

She turned away from the route to the cottages and headed back to the bookshop, slipping in the back door and up to her apartment. She kept the lights low, poured herself a glass of wine, and went to sit in the window.

The town still went on. Couples walking by. A lone runner. The world flowing past her as if Evelyn hadn't just been struck down by a car. Life seemed fragile tonight. It all could be taken away in an instant. And what she had done so far in her life—which she *was* proud of—that was all she'd have when she left this life. She had no children. No family to mourn her. No one but a handful of friends.

Loneliness wrapped around her like a misty fog rolling in from the sea. She sat in the window, sipped her wine, and contemplated her life and the decisions she'd made that had led her to this moment. What had changed? Why was she feeling so lonely now? So... unsettled?

CHAPTER 15

Rob sat beside Evelyn at the hospital. She was way too pale and her breathing shallow. He held one of her hands in his. Those capable hands that were so deft when she worked in the kitchen lay limp and fragile now. He squeezed her hand gently, wanting to give her his strength. He wanted to ease away the wrinkle between her eyes as she winced in pain in her sleep.

He glanced at his watch. The doctors were waiting on test results, but the minutes dragged on as he sat, waiting for them to come in and talk to him. To tell him she would be just fine. *Really* fine. She'd be okay. Not that she needed surgery, or worse.

Machines chirped and beeped. He wanted to reach out and smash them to the floor, silence them. They just reminded him Evelyn was not okay. Not awake.

Evelyn's sister, Donna, came into the room and he glanced up. She crossed over and pressed a cup of coffee into his grasp. She stood beside him, her hand on his shoulder. "Any news yet?"

"No, not yet."

Donna moved beside the bed and brushed back Evelyn's hair. "Evie, wake up, honey. It's all going to be okay."

"They gave her something for the pain a while ago. I'm not sure when it will wear off."

Donna nodded. "That's for the best. She probably needs her rest."

An ugly bruise was forming on her forehead. The nurses had cleaned the blood away and said no stitches were needed. But he was worried about the internal damage he'd heard the doctors discussing.

He should have been watching where they were going. Never let her step out in the street like that. If only the twins hadn't called out. He should have been beside Evelyn, and maybe he could have protected her. He wasn't there for her when she needed him. He would never forgive himself.

Donna turned back to him. "She'll be okay. I know she will. She's a fighter."

"What if she doesn't recover? Isn't okay?" He looked at Donna as pain surged through him, strangling him. "I just… I just can't bear to think about…"

"Then don't." Donna held up her hand, her voice firm and full of confidence. "She's going to be okay. We Parker women are a strong bunch."

The door opened again, and the room was suddenly filled with Evelyn's family. Livy and Emily, Donna's daughter and granddaughter, hurried in and stood by the bed. "Hey, Aunt Evelyn, we're here. Right here with you," Livy said as her mom wrapped an arm around her waist.

The door opened again and Evelyn's mother, Patricia, came in. She crossed the floor, her heels clicking on the floor. She nodded at everyone, then stood regally at the end of the bed, staring at Evelyn, as if not knowing what she should do. What she could do. He knew the feeling well.

The door flew open once again, and Evelyn's daughter, Heather, flew into the room. She hurried to the bedside, her face pale. "Oh, Mom." She took Evelyn's other hand in hers and leaned over and kissed Evelyn's cheek. "What did you always teach me about looking both ways before crossing the street?" she whispered, her voice cracking.

He felt a bit excluded from the family, knowing he wasn't one of them. Like he didn't exactly belong. But there was no way he was leaving Evelyn's side. It felt like she was *his* family. And that thought shocked him. But Evelyn was everything to him. Everything.

The Parker women surrounded Evelyn's bed like a formidable force against her injuries. Arms around each other, sending her their energy. She moaned slightly and opened her eyes. Closed them, then opened them again. She looked at him and gently squeezed his hand. That was a good sign, right?

She slowly looked around the circle of family surrounding her. She licked her lips. "What, did you—" She paused and took a breath. "Did you decide to hold a Parker women brunch without me?"

Was that the tiniest smile on her lips?

Donna laughed and touched her cheek. "No, sweetie, we're waiting for you to get better."

"Oh, Mom." Heather's eyes filled with tears. "I'm so sorry this happened. But you're going to be okay."

"Of course I will," Evelyn said quietly, but with a gentle strength to her words.

A nurse walked into the room, efficiently checking a machine by the bed before turning to the crowd of family. "I think our patient needs her rest. Maybe you all should leave and let her sleep." But it wasn't a suggestion, more like an order.

Evelyn held onto his hand. "Don't leave."

"I won't," he assured her. "I'll stay."

"Okay, one person. But the others need to leave." The nurse bustled over to check another one of the annoying machines.

"Rob should stay. We'll all go and let Evelyn rest." Donna leaned over and kissed the top of Evelyn's head. "Rest and get better."

The women each kissed Evelyn goodbye and disappeared out the door, along with the nurse.

He reached out and touched Evelyn's face. "You scared me."

"I'll be okay."

"Hey, I'm the one who is supposed to be comforting you."

She smiled slightly as she closed her eyes and drifted off to sleep. An hour later, he was still sitting at her side, still watching her. He wanted to never take his eyes off her again.

He answered text messages from what seemed like a hundred people checking in on Evelyn. He convinced Violet to stay at the cottages, that Evelyn needed her sleep.

After what felt like an eternity, but probably was only another hour, the doctor came in and walked over to the bed. "She's a lucky lady. We don't find any sign of internal injuries. She twisted her ankle, but it's not broken. She'll need crutches for a while. And she's going to be very sore and bruised."

Relief swept through him. She was going to be okay. Evelyn was going to be fine. He blinked his eyes rapidly, fighting back tears.

Evelyn stirred and opened her eyes. "Hey, doc." Just like nothing had ever happened.

"Evelyn, I was just telling Rob. You're going

to be fine. No serious damage, but you're going to feel like…" The doctor smiled. "Well, like you got hit by a car."

She shifted slightly in the bed and grimaced. "I do feel like that."

"We want to keep you overnight, just to be cautious. And I can send you home with some pain meds tomorrow, but I don't think you should be alone."

"She won't be." He was not letting her out of his sight.

"Great. I'll check on you in the morning before we release you." The doctor walked out the door.

He stared at her, relieved. But she still looked so pale. "I was so worried. Don't ever do this to me again."

She gave him a weak smile. "I won't." Her forehead wrinkled as she moved again.

"Do you want me to see if they can give you some more pain meds?"

"No, I'm fine. I don't like how they make me feel. Woozy." She closed her eyes. "I'm a bit tired. I think I might… just… rest."

He continued to stay by her side as the night darkened outside. She finally awakened again and smiled as soon as she saw him. "You're still here."

"I'm here. I'm not leaving."

"You should go home and get some rest."

"I'm not leaving," he repeated.

She shook her head, then winced. "I know better than to argue with you when you get your mind set."

"And another thing we need to talk about if you're up to it." He leaned closer.

"I'm fine. Really. What do you want to talk about?"

"I need to ask you something."

She waited patiently, searching his face.

"Life is short. We don't know how long we have on this earth... what might happen." He paused and grabbed her hand. "Marry me. I don't want to waste another day without you. I want to spend every minute with you."

Her eyes widened.

"I love you. I can't imagine my life without you. I know my timing is lousy. Or maybe it's perfect. Will you marry me?"

She broke into a wide smile, tears filling her eyes. "Yes, I'll marry you."

He jumped up in excitement, then plopped

right back down, grabbing her hand again. "Great. Soon. Let's elope tomorrow when you get released."

"My family would kill me."

"Fair point. Okay, then next weekend?"

She looked at him for a moment and her lips curved into a smile, as intimate as a kiss. Her eyes held a glimmer of amusement at his impatience. "Yes, next weekend."

"Really?" He stared at her in amazement.

"Really. Though, my family is still going to kill me."

CHAPTER 16

Rob drove over to the cottages early the next day. If Violet found out he was getting married from someone besides him—like the Jenkins twins—she'd kill him. He picked up a half dozen muffins from Sea Glass Cafe. He hoped they would soften the news when he explained things. Explained he was getting married *next weekend*. He could hardly believe it himself.

He walked through the door, balancing the box of muffins. "Hey, sis."

She rolled her eyes at him, which was not unexpected. "You checking on me again?" She reached for the box. "But come in and tell me all about Evelyn. How's she doing? I thought you'd be at the hospital bright and early this morning."

"I was there all night. Slept in the chair. Just ran home and changed clothes. Heading there right after here."

"But you thought you had to pop in and check on me first?" She opened the box and snagged a muffin.

"I... uh, no. That's not it."

"Evelyn is okay, right? Or she will be. Just banged up you said."

"Yes, Evelyn will be fine. Better than fine. You see..." He took a deep breath. "I've asked her to marry me and she said yes."

"Of course, she did." Violet set the muffin down and hugged him. "Congrats, Robbie. I'm very happy for you."

"There's a bit more to it." He eyed her, knowing he was probably going to get an earful when she heard they wanted the wedding next weekend.

"Then spill it." She stood with her hands on her hips, facing him.

"We're getting married... next weekend."

"You're what?" Her hands flew to her mouth.

"We don't want to wait. I almost lost her, sis. I can't waste any more time."

Her eyes narrowed. "And Evelyn agreed to this?"

"She did."

Violet's lips spread into a grin as she shook her head. "Okay, then. Looks like we have a busy week ahead of us. I'll help in any way I can."

Relief swept through him at her eager acceptance. "Well, there is one thing. I looked on your online calendar—I still have the login because you're always messing something up and asking me to fix it."

"I do not." She glared at him, then laughed. "Okay, maybe I do. But you can fix techie things so much quicker than I can."

"Anyway, as I was saying. You don't have a wedding scheduled for next weekend."

She clapped her hands. "And you want to have it here? That would be great. We can do this."

"Really, you're okay with it on such short notice?"

"Of course. It's not every day my big brother gets married." She grabbed a piece of paper. "We need to plan. I need to know how many people are coming. What color ribbons on the chairs. How many serving tables."

"I'll get you all of that info after I talk to Evelyn again. I'm just heading out to get her from the hospital and take her back to my place. I don't want her alone after all this."

"Don't blame you." Violet scribbled a note. "So get back to me this afternoon. I'm going to weed the courtyard, too. So it's all cleaned up." She jotted on the paper again. "Oh, and find out if she wants flowers on the arbor."

"I'll talk to her."

She grabbed her phone. "Which day?"

"Saturday, I think?"

"Oh, look." She held out her phone. "Perfect weather."

He hadn't even thought to check the weather. What if they predicted rain? They couldn't have it outside in the courtyard if it rained. "Oh, good." One less detail to worry about. "And one more thing."

"What's that?" She stood with her pen poised above the paper.

"Would you... would you be my best man?"

She grinned at him. "Of course I will be. Who else would be the best man?"

He hugged her quickly. "You really are the best," he said gruffly, filled with emotion.

She smacked his arm lightly and stepped back. "Go pick up Evelyn. I'll start getting things organized here. How about flowers and food and her dress?"

He looked at Violet. Yes, all those things. He hadn't thought of all those details when he'd proposed and wanted the wedding so soon. Was Evelyn really okay with all of this? "I… I'll have to check with Evelyn. I guess I didn't think of all the things that would need to be done."

She laughed. "Of course you didn't. You just want to be married to her. Nothing wrong with that. We'll figure it out. I'll do everything I can to help."

He gave her a quick hug. "You're my favorite sister."

"Your only sister." She stepped back and shooed him. "Go. Pick up Evelyn. Make some plans. Then let me know what I can do to help."

"Will do." He ducked out the door and loped to his car. He couldn't wait to see Evelyn.

161

They'd figure this all out. Get it all planned. Somehow.

Evelyn wasn't used to someone fussing over her like this. Rob had practically carried her in from the car and settled her onto the couch at his cottage. He'd insisted that his cottage was a better place for her to recover than her apartment. Fair observation—his cottage had no steps except off the deck to the beach. It surprised her how much better she felt today than last night. Sore, of course. And bruises covered one whole side of her body. Not to mention she had an ugly bruise on her forehead that she'd spied in the mirror. She wasn't sure how she'd be able to cover that up for the wedding.

The wedding. Where? When? How would she pull it off by next weekend? Today was Friday. So she had one week. Though, to be honest, if it wouldn't hurt her family's feelings so much, she would have taken Rob up on his suggestion to elope. But they'd never forgive her for eloping.

Somehow she was going to pull this off because she wanted nothing more than to be married to Rob. He was right. Life is short. This accident had thrown that fact in her face. She'd been very lucky to survive with fairly minor injuries. She eyed the crutches leaning against the wall. And she hoped she'd be off those by the weekend.

Rob came into the room, carrying a cup of hot tea. "Here you go. Just the way you like it, I hope." He set it on the coffee table by her.

"You can quit fussing over me. I'm really okay." She reached for the tea. She was used to taking care of him. Fixing him meals. She couldn't remember the last time someone had taken care of *her*.

A knock sounded, and Rob went to open the door. Donna, Livy, and Heather hurried in, carrying a bouquet, a large picnic basket, and a suitcase.

"I picked up some things for you from your apartment." Donna set the suitcase down.

"Melody packed up some meals for you." Livy handed the basket to Rob.

"Do you have a vase? I brought these flowers for Mom." Heather handed the flowers to Rob, who disappeared into the kitchen and returned with the flowers in a vase.

She rearranged them slightly when he set them on the table before her. She couldn't help herself. He'd just crammed them in there. He noticed and grinned.

"So, you're feeling better?" Heather sat down beside her.

"I am. Much."

"You've got your color back." Donna frowned. "You actually look… like you're glowing." Donna leaned over and placed a hand on her forehead. "No, no fever."

"I'm fine." She turned to Livy. "Everything going okay at the cafe? I hate leaving you shorthanded."

"Last night Collette and Ethan jumped in and helped Melody. Emily is taking on more shifts. We're good. You just rest and feel better."

"About that rest thing…"

The three Parker women froze and stared at her.

"What?" Donna eyed her suspiciously.

Rob perched on the arm of the sofa and draped an arm around her in support.

"Ah… I'm getting married this coming weekend."

"What?" Donna's eyes flew open.

"Mom, you can't. You're not up to that. You just got hit by a car." Heather shook her head, frowning.

"Wait, Rob asked you to marry him?" Livy looked at her and then Rob and then back at her.

"I did. And she said yes. We decided we didn't want to wait."

"Hey, I turned down his suggestion that we elope today as soon as I left the hospital."

"Okay then," Donna said.

Livy and Heather stared at her, their mouths agape.

"If that's what Evie wants, that's what we'll do." She nodded firmly. "We can do this. Seems like we Parker women are always pulling off quick weddings. First, we need a venue."

"We have one. I talked to Violet this morning. We're going to have it at the cottages. Next Saturday evening."

"That gives us a week to pull this off. Nothing fancy. Simple. And I just want a small wedding. Just family and a few friends." She looked at her sister. "I mean it. Small. Just the ceremony, then cake and champagne afterward."

"Are you sure?" Heather asked.

She took her daughter's hand. "I've never been more sure about anything in my life."

"Well, then. Let's get to work. I'll arrange for the cake." Livy plopped down in the chair next to the sofa.

"I could bake it," she suggested.

"You're not baking your own cake." Livy shook her head. "I'll see if Melody will make it. Vanilla, right? Your favorite?"

She looked at Rob, who nodded in agreement. "Yes, vanilla."

"I'll arrange for the flowers." Heather took out her phone and tapped in a list.

"Just a bouquet for me. White flowers. Then maybe an arrangement for the cake table."

"That's it?" Heather asked.

"Yes. Simple. Casual. All I care about is saying I do to Rob."

"My kind of wedding." Rob grinned. "And I already talked to Violet. We'll set up the chairs and string lights on the arbor. Evelyn wants to get married at sunset."

"So that's about seven-thirty?" Heather started searching on her phone.

"Seven-eighteen." Rob laughed. "I already looked it up."

"So I thought we'd start the ceremony at seven." She smiled at Rob. "A short ceremony."

"I've already talked to the pastor. And we'll apply for our license on Monday at city hall." Rob's eyes twinkled. "I'm trying to do as much as possible to make it easy on Evelyn."

"What about a dress?" Heather tapped some more onto her phone, adding to her list.

"I… I don't know. I just want something simple, not a real wedding-ish dress."

"We'll go shopping tomorrow in Sarasota if you're feeling up to it. We'll find a perfect dress. I promise." Heather tapped more into her phone.

"I'm coming, too," Donna insisted. "Wouldn't miss it for anything."

"I'd come, but I think I'll be holding down the fort at Parker's," Livy said.

"You know, let's close Parker's and the cafe at noon next Saturday. There should be some advantages to owning the place." Donna laughed. "Oh, and we need to tell Mother."

"I'll call her this afternoon." She hoped her mom wouldn't be upset by the short notice. But hadn't that been the Parker women's style for the last few weddings?

Heather stood. "I'm going to head over to Belle Island and see what will be available from Flossie's Flower Shop."

"Too bad the new floral shop here in Moonbeam isn't open yet," Livy said.

"Are you sure you're up for all of this?" Donna's forehead creased. "You just got out of the hospital."

"A little hospital stay isn't going to keep me from marrying Rob. I might need a bit of makeup help, though. This bruise isn't going away anytime soon."

"We'll fix it so no one even knows it's there." Heather bent over and kissed her forehead. "Get some rest. We'll take care of everything."

"Thanks, honey. I'll see you tomorrow?"

"I'll pick you up at eleven."

"Livy, we should go, too. We've got a lot to do." Donna gathered her things. "Rest. Don't overdo it."

"I won't."

They all left, and she reached for her now

lukewarm tea. She took a sip anyway, then leaned back on the sofa. "My family is wonderful. But they can be a bit overwhelming at times." She smiled. "But I guess that's good because it sounds like we're going to have this whole wedding sorted out in no time."

"You sure you're good with having it so quickly? I really want to marry you as soon as possible, but I don't want you to regret it later. Afraid you missed out on something."

She looked up and touched his face. "I'm not missing anything. I'm happy to just be marrying you. We'll have a lovely wedding, I just know it."

He kissed her gently. "I'd marry you anywhere, anytime. I love you. I was so afraid I would lose you."

"You won't lose me." She smiled. "Looks like you're stuck with me forever."

"Can't imagine it any other way." He kissed her again.

CHAPTER 17

Collette decided to go to Violet's happy hour. Feeling like a bit of a rebel, she left the shop a little before five. She wanted to check on Mark. Make sure he was okay after whatever that was yesterday. His episode.

She walked over to Blue Heron Cottages, enjoying the nice weather they were having. The town moved a bit more slowly in September and October. Kids back in school. Fewer tourists, which wasn't great for business at her store, but it was a nice break. And when they were lucky, perfect weather like today. Sunshine, low humidity, and a slight breeze.

She walked past the office and into the courtyard. Violet and Rose stood by a table with the drinks and appetizers. She scanned the crowd, but no sign of Mark. Crossing the distance, she glanced over at his cottage. He wasn't out on his porch either. He didn't know she was coming, so he wasn't avoiding her, she assured herself.

"Hey, Collette. Glad you could come. Did you hear the big news?" Violet asked.

"About Evelyn's accident?"

"Well, that. But other big news. Rob and Evelyn are getting married. This coming weekend."

"Oh, that's wonderful news. So Evelyn is feeling okay? That was a really scary accident yesterday."

"It was. She's banged up a bit, but she'll be fine."

"I can see why an incident like that would make you reassess your life. Decide what you want from it." Rose sipped on a glass of wine. "I'm happy for them."

"That doesn't give them much time to plan it." She reached for a glass of wine.

"I'm helping. And of course I'm sure Donna and Livy and Heather will, too. It's going to be here."

"That sounds wonderful." She took a sip of the wine and glanced over at Mark's cottage again.

Violet laughed. "He said he was coming to happy hour." She nodded toward his cottage.

Just then, the door opened, and Mark stepped out. He was dressed in khaki shorts and a sky-blue shirt. He looked more relaxed this time. Different than last week's happy hour. He'd tanned up this past week, too. He looked… strikingly handsome. He paused on the top step, saw them looking at him, and waved.

He stepped off the porch and strode across toward them. Not the tentative steps of last week. It looked like he was becoming used to being here. More comfortable.

"Ladies." He nodded when he got there.

"Beer's in the tub over there." Violet motioned to the washtub brimming with ice, beer, and soda.

He grabbed one, twisted off the top, and took a swig as he turned back to them. "Nice turnout."

"The cottages are full this weekend," Violet said.

"Then there are the townspeople who come and crash happy hour." Collette laughed.

"You're always welcome. Love seeing you here." Violet turned to greet a new couple.

Collette turned to Mark. "So, you're all good?"

"I'm fine."

"Yesterday—"

"I'm fine, really. It was nothing."

So he wasn't going to explain it. Okay then. He had his secrets. The Jenkins twins came up to the group. "Oh, Violet, you're always asking us to stop by. So we decided to take you up on your offer," Jackie said.

"Yes, we did." Jillian nodded. "We're glad you fixed up the resort and wanted to show our support."

"Thanks for coming." Violet handed each a glass of wine.

"So you all heard about Evelyn." Jackie shook her head. "So sad."

"We saw the whole accident, you know. We were right there."

"She was so pale. It was frightening."

The twins bringing up the accident just made her remember how Mark had reacted.

And the fact that he obviously didn't want to talk about it.

"But look how it turned out. They're getting married this coming weekend." Jackie took a sip of her wine.

"Yes, it all worked out, didn't it? Evelyn is a lucky woman." Jillian clinked her glass with Jackie's.

Naturally, the twins had already heard the news and were spreading it around town. She smiled at them both. Gossips, but good-hearted ones. They looked genuinely pleased for Evelyn and Rob.

She and Mark stood and chatted with Rose and Violet and different guests as they came out to enjoy happy hour and the wonderful weather. At the end, they helped Violet bring in the leftover drinks and take down the table.

After they finished, she and Mark stood alone outside the office. "I guess I should go." She was not going to ask him to get dinner with her. Or do anything. She wasn't.

"Would you like to go for a beach walk first?" He stood looking at her. "You know, if you have time."

"I'd love to." Ha, she hadn't asked him.

He'd asked *her*. Maybe he wasn't really avoiding her and it was all in her mind because of her past? Because of the mistake she'd made? Unwilling to get lost in her thoughts, just wanting to enjoy the walk, she put it out of her mind as they crossed the courtyard together.

They headed toward the beach, kicked off their shoes under a palm, and strolled down to the shoreline. They walked along with the water lapping around their ankles in foamy stacks of saltwater.

She decided to try one more time. "Yesterday when Evelyn was hurt…"

He stopped and turned to her. "Want to sit for a bit?"

She nodded and dropped down on the sand. He sat beside her, almost touching, and sent her a look, a cross between a weak smile and a grimace. "Okay, I'll explain. So… a few months ago…"

CHAPTER 18

The last thing he wanted to do was to actually talk about what happened. But Collette had been concerned when he freaked out yesterday. Heck, *he'd* been concerned. It had been so hard to catch his breath, and his pulsed roared through his veins. The room spun in a crazy whirlwind. And when it was over, he'd felt so foolish.

You're a dumb scaredy-cat. His brother's voice echoed in his mind.

But what would she think when she heard what he'd done? It was all his fault, no matter what Mr. Mason said.

He took a deep breath and plunged into the story. "I said I worked at the hardware store."

She nodded.

"One night a few weeks ago, I had a date. I don't have dates very often. I was supposed to close the store that night, and the date was afterward." He paused, looking out at the water. "I was supposed to close... but I didn't. The high school kid who works there, Ian, offered to close. And I let him. But it was my responsibility. Ian told me I needed to go home and change clothes before my date—and he was right—but I should have stayed."

She sat silently by his side, watching him closely.

"I went to the stupid date. It was at the diner in town. All dressed in my nice clothes. It was a setup. I only agreed to it because it was arranged by my boss, Mr. Mason. Anyway, the woman... she never showed up."

She frowned.

"No, that's not the problem. See, after she ghosted me, I finally left and went outside. I saw flashing lights and heard sirens." He closed his eyes and swallowed, chasing away the memory etched in his brain. "They were in front of the hardware store. I raced down the street in a panic. When I got there, I rushed inside. Shelves were tipped over. Merchandise scattered around. And then I saw him. On the floor. Blood all around him. I thought he was dead. The EMTs were all around him."

She put her hand over his and nodded as if telling him to go on.

"Turns out, right before closing, a man came in. Demanded money. There was a struggle. Ian was shot multiple times. The shot to his leg did a lot of damage." He dug a heel in the sand, scraping a trough below his foot.

"Oh, that's horrible. No child should ever have to worry about being shot at work. Or anywhere."

He nodded. "I know. He had to have surgery. Then another one. He was the star quarterback and missed the big game. There were college scouts there. He was hoping for a scholarship. But now, he probably won't even be ready to play next year. And I'm not sure he'll make it to college without a scholarship."

"That's really too bad." Her eyes were filled with sympathy. "So you feel like it's your fault because things might have been different if you'd still been there?"

He nodded.

"I can see how you'd feel that way. It's not really your fault, but a decision you made affected someone else." She squeezed his hand. "I get it."

He stared at her. She understood him. How he felt. It had been a litany of people telling him it wasn't his fault, but no one understood—up until now—how he still did feel responsible.

"And does Ian blame you?"

"No." He shook his head. "But I blame me. I was the one who was supposed to be working until closing that night."

"We all make choices in life. They sometimes affect other people. But there was no way you could have known your choice that night would end up like it did. I do understand your guilt, though. That you wished things would have worked out differently. Though, we eventually have to learn to make peace with our choices."

"He's so young. And he has a long recovery ahead of him. He was hoping to play college football next year. But I don't think that will happen." Guilt swept through him again.

"So, you're going to let that one decision—that you never knew would turn out like it did—

overshadow everything good you've done in your life?"

"I don't think I've done a lot of good in my life."

"Why would you say that?"

Because it had been hammered into his head from day one that he was a loser. He was dumb. Stupid. Never did anything right. And his mother had been correct. He hadn't done the right thing that night when Ian was injured. Ian must have been so scared lying there on the floor, bleeding, all alone.

"You know that the blame really lies with the man who did this to Ian, right?" she asked softly.

"Logically, I know that. But I still feel guilty. If only I had been there."

"Focusing on if-only is a difficult way to live."

Maybe. But how did he get past it? That was the million-dollar question.

"So now when you hear sirens?"

"It's like a flashback, and all I can see is Ian on the floor. Pale. All that blood." He wiped a hand over his face. "And the look of horror on his mom's face when she got to the scene. How helpless I felt. I still feel."

"That's understandable."

"But I can't go through life feeling like I'm going to pass out every time I hear a siren or see flashing lights."

"No, you can't. But I would hope it would get less and less over time." She paused and looked at him. "Or after you find a way to forgive yourself."

He wasn't sure that would ever happen.

Collette sat quietly beside Mark, her hand still covering his. At least she understood his panic when he heard the sirens. It was awful what happened to Ian. It was. But it wasn't really Mark's fault. Although she could certainly see how he'd feel guilty about not being there.

Maybe he would feel better after telling her all of this. She felt closer to him now. Like she understood him better. And she understood that haunted look hiding at the corners of his eyes.

A long sigh escaped him as he stared out at

the water. That was probably a good sign, right? Maybe he was starting to make peace with it all?

They sat in silence for a while as the sky darkened and stars began to glitter in the sky above them. There was something so intimate about sitting here under the stars with no one in sight and the sea rolling to shore, its waves breaking into foaming white splashes in the moonlight.

He finally turned to her. "Thanks for listening. I haven't told anyone about it. How I felt about it, I mean."

"Sometimes it helps to talk and get it out in the open."

He nodded. "Sometimes. I just don't want you to…"

"To what?"

"To think less of me. Knowing what I did."

She reached over and touched his face, surprised that a flash of electricity surged through her at the gesture. "I don't think less of you. I think *more* of you. That you feel so deeply for Ian. That you care about him and feel for him and what he's going through. Empathy is a good quality, one that so many people don't seem to have these days."

Gratitude shone in his eyes. "Thank you. I think… I *know* I needed to hear that."

"You're a good man, Mark Wheeler, and I'm glad I've gotten this chance to get to know you. Sometimes life gives us a chance to meet someone who… who we're supposed to meet. Supposed to get to know. Like fate or something."

He slowly placed his arm around her shoulder and drew her close to his side. "I'm glad fate decided to have me meet you." Then he kissed the top of her head.

Her heart pounded. She hadn't imagined that, had she? Maybe he'd just bumped his chin against her head. No, he'd kissed her. Okay, the top of her head, but still. That counted, didn't it? And how did she feel about that? She turned her head and looked up at him. He stared back at her, and for a minute she was certain he was going to kiss her. A real kiss.

But he just gave her a smile and turned back to look at the water.

Maybe she was crazy and he really had just bumped her head. And maybe he hadn't been ready to kiss her a moment ago. Maybe she was imagining the whole thing.

They sat like that for a long time. Side by side, watching the waves roll in under the twinkling stars. She hadn't felt this at peace with life in a very long, long time. At peace, but with an undercurrent of wondering if he really had been getting ready to kiss her.

CHAPTER 19

The next morning Mark headed into town. He had to admit he felt lighter than he had in weeks. It was so nice to finally talk to someone about how he felt about that night Ian got hurt. And she understood his guilt, his feelings. She was right that he should make peace with it, though. Ian didn't blame him. Mr. Mason didn't.

It was just him. He blamed himself.

He didn't really have plans for his day. Just wander around town a bit and see what caught his attention. He might pop into Collette's shop—for some tea and cookies, not to see her. Oh, who was he kidding? Of course it was to see her. Last night, he'd felt so close to her. He'd almost kissed her but stopped himself. He had no idea how she felt about him. They'd only known each other for a little over a week now. And really, she was so accomplished. Well-read. Traveled the world. Beautiful. He could list off a million things that held them apart.

He pushed the thoughts aside and decided to go to Parker's General Store. It wasn't really a hardware store like Mason's, but he still was interested to see what it was like.

He crossed the street and pushed through the door to Parker's. A woman with a welcoming smile greeted him. "Good morning. Welcome to Parker's."

"Morning."

"What can I help you find?"

"I'm not sure. I just wanted to come in and see the store. Then I might treat myself to breakfast at Sea Glass Cafe."

"Melody made cinnamon rolls today. I'm Donna, by the way."

"Nice to meet you, Donna."

"Browse around and let me know if I can help you."

He wandered the aisles, looking at how they'd organized the merchandise. He would have done some of them differently, but he did like how they had a well-sorted section of phone cords, chargers, and cases. He made a mental note to do that at Mason's. Why hadn't he thought of a section of those?

He walked through the opening from the general store to the cafe and got a table. A young girl, maybe about sixteen or so and full of energy, came up to the table. "Hi, welcome to Sea Glass Cafe." She handed him a menu. "I'm Emily. Oh, and the cinnamon rolls are great here. Melody is just pulling another batch out of the oven."

"You've sold me. A cinnamon roll and coffee, please."

Emily hurried away, stopped at a nearby table for a minute and spoke to the couple sitting there, then headed into the kitchen. He could smell the enticing aroma of cinnamon and yeast drifting through the cafe.

A man came in—he was sure he'd met him at Violet's—what was his name?

Violet. Rose. Collette. Melody. Ethan. The names he'd memorized at the first happy hour popped into his mind. Ethan, that was it.

Ethan stopped at his table. "Morning. Mark, isn't it? Met you at Violet's."

"Ethan, hi. I just stopped in for what I hear are delicious cinnamon rolls."

"Word is out. Melody made fresh rolls today." Ethan grinned. "I came in for one myself."

"Care to join me?" His offer surprised him. It wasn't like him to ask a stranger to join him.

"Sure." Ethan dropped into the seat across from him.

Emily came back with his coffee and turned to Ethan. "Ethan, morning. Coffee, black?"

"Yes, please, and a cinnamon roll."

Emily grinned. "The twins were in early this morning and had the cinnamon rolls. By now, I'm sure half the town knows Melody made them today. We've sold a ton of them this morning." She went and got coffee for Ethan, then went to wait on another table filled with high-school-aged kids talking and laughing.

The anticipation of the cinnamon roll was killing him. His stomach growled as he picked up his coffee cup and took a sip.

"So, are you enjoying your vacation?" Ethan asked.

"I am. Doing a bit of exploring. Taking time to read some books. Well, listen to books."

"Ah, I'm an audiobook fan myself. Dyslexic, so reading is hard for me. But with the audiobook, I can just get lost in it without any struggles."

He stared at Ethan in amazement. He'd just blurted out he was dyslexic with absolutely no sign of embarrassment or excuse. How did he do that?

Before he knew what he was doing, for the first time, he was divulging his own deep, dark secret. The one his mother told him to never tell anyone or they'd think he was stupid. The one the teachers had known but that he tried so hard to hide from anyone else. "Ah, I'm dyslexic, too. And I just discovered audiobooks. Don't know what took me so long."

"Great way to devour books, isn't it? Have you read any of Rob Bentley's books?"

"I just finished his newest one last week. So good. I swear I did nothing but listen to that book for hours on end. I couldn't wait to hear how it finished, but then, I was kind of sorry it ended."

Ethan laughed. "I felt exactly the same way."

Melody came out of the kitchen carrying two plates of cinnamon rolls. "Gentlemen, your breakfast."

"Thanks." He reached for his.

"Uh, hi, Melody." Ethan stared at Melody, barely taking his eyes off her.

"Ethan, I knew you'd be in when you heard I made cinnamon rolls. Luckily, I made a double batch." She smiled at both of them, but her gaze lingered a bit longer on Ethan. Or maybe he was imagining it.

He took a bite. "This is wonderful."

"Thanks. Evelyn taught me how to make them. I use her recipe. I still say hers are better, but I'm almost there."

"You're great." Ethan blurted out, his cheeks reddening. "I mean, the rolls are great. As good as Evelyn's or better."

She laughed. "Thank you. I better go back to the kitchen. Just wanted to say hi."

Ethan watched Melody as she left, the spots of red still highly visible on his cheekbones. Was there something there between Melody and Ethan?

"So, Melody. She seems nice." He watched for Ethan's reaction.

"She is." Ethan looked down quickly and took a bite of his roll.

"Have you known her long?"

"Ever since she came to town. About ten years or so ago."

"Single?"

"Who, Melody? She's a widow."

"Oh, that's too bad. Recent?"

"Been a few years now."

"That's tough being a widow so young."

Ethan nodded.

"And you're dating Melody?"

"What, no. Just friends." Ethan shook his head vehemently.

They'd looked like more than friends when he'd seen them together at happy hour and here at the cafe. But what did he know? "Oh, I guess I got that wrong."

"Yes, Melody is… wonderful. She's smart, pretty, funny. Everyone loves her." He shook his head. "She wouldn't be interested in someone like me."

"You never know."

"I'm not even in her league."

Ethan's words rang in his ears. Hadn't he said the exact same thing about Collette? That he wasn't in her league?

"Besides, like I said. Melody is a widow. She was so in love with her husband. They were the perfect couple, and he was a great guy. Funny. Kind. Always lending a helping hand to anyone who needed it. And he could tell a joke that would have the entire room laughing. He was just so outgoing, sociable, and full of life. Different than me."

"But you'd like to ask her out?" He eyed Ethan.

"I… I've thought about it. I doubt she'd say yes. And you saw Melody. She's beautiful. I'm just a boring old insurance guy."

He chewed his bottom lip. Here was Ethan, thinking he didn't measure up. But he did. He seemed like a genuinely nice guy. "I think you should ask her out."

"I couldn't." Ethan shook his head again.

"Why not?"

"Because… because… what if she said no? It would just be so awkward then."

"What if she said yes?" He leaned back in

his chair. He had a strong feeling that she would.

"I don't know…"

"Well, I think you should think about it."

Ethan sat silently as he finished his cinnamon roll with no less than a dozen glances back toward the kitchen. It was too bad Ethan thought he wasn't good enough for Melody. Of course, he thought the exact same thing about him and Collette. That she was smart, well-read, traveled, and exceptionally good-looking. And he was just his plain old self.

He and Ethan were quite the pair.

CHAPTER 20

Mark left the cafe and headed to Beachside Bookshop. He pushed inside and saw Collette was sitting in a corner, surrounded by kids. He glanced over at a sign saying story hour. Ah, he'd come at the wrong time.

She looked up, smiled, and waved. He browsed around the shop but didn't want to bother her. He wandered out to the courtyard and had some tea. A few other customers came out, but no one he knew. Not that he knew very many people in town.

The story hour broke up and he waited for the crowd of mothers and kids to leave. Right as he was walking up to say hi to Collette, the worker at the desk—he thought Collette had said her name was Jody—called out, "Collette, can you come help Mr. Hamilton? He heard there's a new book out with photos of Florida's old hotels. And The Cabot Hotel is supposed to be in it."

Collette hurried over to the desk.

He picked out a magazine to buy. He couldn't just lurk around the shop all day and buy nothing. He went over to check out, but Collette and Mr. Hamilton had disappeared into the back of the shop. After paying for the magazine, he couldn't think of a reason to hang around any longer—you know, except to see Collette—but he'd already been here over an hour.

He slipped outside, disappointed that he hadn't had a chance to talk to Collette. But really, she was working. He shouldn't be bothering her.

He wandered around town a bit, went in and out of a few stores, and ended up buying a Moonbeam Bay t-shirt. It would remind him of the place after he left.

After he left.

He was no longer in any hurry to return to

Summerville. Now that was a huge change, wasn't it? When did that happen? Slowly over the last week?

After he returned to his cottage, he downloaded another book by Rob Bentley and sat out on his porch, listening to it. Soon his mind wandered, back to contemplating why he wasn't eager to return home, and he shut off the audiobook. He stood up and stretched.

If he was honest—and he wasn't sure he was ready to be—he knew why he wasn't eager to leave. Collette. One hundred percent it was Collette. He enjoyed getting to know her. His pulse quickened when he saw her and the smile she always had at the ready. The way he could talk to her about everything. Well, almost anything.

His thoughts popped back to the way Ethan had just nonchalantly mentioned he was dyslexic. How did a person get to that stage? Where they could just blurt that out. *Don't tell anyone. They'll know you're not smart.* His mother's voice bounced around his mind.

He frowned. It wasn't really that he wasn't smart. He just had a disability that made some things harder for him.

Keep saying that, Mark, and maybe someday you'll believe it.

Collette was sorry she'd been so busy and had missed getting a chance to talk to Mark when he was in the shop. She'd looked for him after Delbert Hamilton left, but Jody said Mark was gone. Why had he left without at least chatting with her a bit? She must have been wrong when she thought he was getting ready to kiss her last night. Because he would have stayed to talk to her, right? If he was interested in her in that way?

You don't date someone who you don't know where you stand with them. Her golden rule. Had she not learned her lesson? But did he even want to date her? She ignored her disappointment and confusion as a steady stream of customers came to the shop.

She closed the store that night and wandered outside. She didn't feel like eating alone upstairs in her apartment. Deciding dinner at Jimmy's on the Wharf was a good plan, she headed in that direction. She'd be eating alone, but at least surrounded by people. She couldn't face the loneliness she felt in her apartment these days.

The wharf was filled with people milling around on this Saturday night. Wandering in and out of shops. Sipping coffee at one of the many sitting areas. She walked to the end of the wharf and into Jimmy's.

"Hi, Collette," Aspen said. "You meeting Mark here?"

"No, just me."

"Oh, because he's here. I just sat him at a table by the railing."

"Just one," she repeated. She was not going to intrude on Mark. Suggest they eat together. Besides, he hadn't stayed to talk to her at her shop today, had he?

Aspen led her through the inside dining and out to the deck. Mark saw her and waved. "Collette, want to join me?" he called out.

Yes, she wanted to join him. There was nothing she wanted more right at this minute. A spontaneous smile spread across her face. Aspen led her to Mark's table and set the menu down. "I'll have your server come right over for your drink orders."

"This is a nice surprise," Mark said.

And was that a welcoming smile on his face? He did seem pleased to see her, didn't he? Why was she feeling so insecure? It didn't sound like he was avoiding her. Why was she so uneasy regarding if he wanted to spend time with her or not?

But she knew the answer to that. She never wanted to be involved with someone and not know where she stood. She'd learned that lesson years ago and didn't plan on making the same mistake again. But was she doing that with Mark? Making a mistake? She didn't really know what they were. Acquaintances? Friends? Just some random kind-of strangers who kept running into each other?

Had he been getting ready to kiss her last night?

"It is a nice surprise," she finally answered as she sat down on the chair across from him. It was almost like fate was playing with them. Throwing them together again and again, no matter what promises she made to herself.

CHAPTER 21

Mark was thrilled that Collette had come to Jimmy's tonight. Fate kept pushing them together, and he sure didn't mind. At least this way, she wouldn't think he was going out of his way to spend time with her. Even though he really wanted to. Spending time at dinner with her suited him just fine. He looked forward to talking with her and watching her enchanting smile. He pulled his glance away from that smile—did she notice he was staring at her?—and made himself look at the menu.

Collette waved to a woman coming in, and the woman came over to the table. "Heather, good to see you. How's your mom doing?" She turned to him. "This is Heather, Evelyn's daughter."

He nodded at her.

"She's doing better. She was so lucky. I've postponed the trip I was going to take to Paris. I wanted to do some sketching there for a new line of cards. I like to get immersed in a subject that I'm working on. But I don't want to leave her now. Not to mention her upcoming wedding."

"I heard she's getting married next weekend. I'm very happy for her and Rob. And Paris. That's too bad to postpone your trip. I love Paris. It's such a romantic place. So much history. And such good food. I love to sit outside at one of the many cafes and people watch."

"It is great, isn't it? That's what made me come up with the idea for this series of cards. There's something magical about the city. I already have a prospective buyer for the series."

He sat there and listened to them chat about Paris. A city he knew nothing about except for seeing it in a few movies. They moved on to talking about Prague. Then castles in Scotland. All of which he'd never seen. He was just a small-town man. Not some world traveler like these two.

Heather left to join her party, and Collette turned back to him. "She's such a nice young woman, isn't she?"

He nodded.

"Younger than I am, but she seems older than her years."

"I'm younger than you. Nine years." He wanted to smack his forehead. What had he just said to her? Why in the world would he blurt that out? He was stupid. Just like his mother always said. Never knowing what to say.

"Really?" she said nonchalantly as if it was no big deal.

Like any woman wanted to be reminded about her age. His mother was always telling him to lie about her age. She'd been thirty-five for about eight years before moving on to being forty-one for another ten years.

"I don't know why I said that." He shook his head. But he did feel like she was older and more experienced, more worldly.

"That's not much of a difference at our ages, is it?" She gave him one of those enchanting smiles that made him feel even more foolish and inadequate. Was she just being kind to him and she was really annoyed at his comment about her age? *Women don't talk about their age.* His mother's voice taunted him.

The conversation was thankfully interrupted by their server bringing their drinks. But he still felt ridiculous for blurting that out. Who says something like that?

They ordered their meals and chatted over dinner, though there were some awkward pauses in the conversation, mostly on his part. Collette talked about the current book she was reading, a memoir about a woman's journey to find herself by taking a trip across the United States. He'd never read a memoir. Another difference between them. He should do an internet search on the book so he could talk intelligently about it if she brought it up again.

He'd finished his meal and his drink, but Collette was still sipping on her wine.

Finally, their server brought the bill, and he reached for it. "I'll get this."

"Oh, we can split it."

"No, I'd like to get it." Not that it would make up for his behavior tonight. The stupid comment about her age. His unease after her conversation with Heather. This whole meal had just brought up how different they were.

He added up the bill and calculated the tip, wishing he could take out his phone and do the math like he usually did, but he didn't want her to think he couldn't even do simple math. He did the math—twice—in his head, then added the tip and totaled it. The server came and took it.

There, now they could leave. The entire night had gone from wanting to spend time with her to needing to get away. He'd felt so inadequate all evening.

Before he could stand, the server came back. "Sir, I noticed your total. I think you reversed these first two numbers. The total doesn't cover the meal now. I don't want you to think I'm cheating you."

The heat of embarrassment flooded his face. "I'm sorry. I was in too much of a hurry, I guess. Here, let me correct it." He quickly corrected the bill, wondering if he still had it right. The server took it, smiled, and left.

Stupid, Mark. You're too dumb to figure out your bill. He swore he could hear both his mother and brother mocking him. He stood up abruptly. "I'm going to leave. But you should stay and finish your wine."

"I… okay." She looked a little confused.

But at this point, he just needed to escape. He'd been wrong in thinking Collette would be interested in a man like him. *You're so dumb. Look at that dumb mistake you made.* His brother's singsong voice mocked him in his mind. His brother was right, he was an idiot.

With that, he turned and fled out of the restaurant, making his escape.

Collette sat and watched Mark practically race out of Jimmy's. What had just happened? He couldn't be upset about the wrong total on the bill, could he? Everyone made an addition mistake at some time in their lives.

She'd hoped he'd walk her home. But he hadn't offered. And their conversation had been awkward at times tonight. Almost like he was… bored with her? Did her constant talk of books bore him? Was that it? She should let him talk more. She vowed to do just that the next time she saw him.

Maybe he was just one of those people who didn't like to dine alone. So he'd asked her to join him. Maybe that was all it was. And the imagined almost kiss last night? Imagined.

She took another sip of her wine. And here she was, uncertain of how she stood with Mark. The one thing she would never let happen. And she certainly would not go chasing after him.

She tried too hard before, long ago. And that had backfired big time. She'd learned her lesson. Pushing away the memories she rarely let herself think of, she took the last sip of her wine and slid out of her chair, determined. That was the last time she'd have a meal with Mark. Do anything with the man. The last thing she needed was to be tangled up with someone who wasn't really interested in her. Who gave off mixed signals. Who raced out of a restaurant after having dinner with her.

There, the decision was made.

She headed down the wharf and onto the sidewalk, heading back to her apartment. She should feel good now that she'd made up her mind. Protected her heart. But loneliness settled around her.

This is what she got for trying to help out a

stranger to their town. Befriending him. Caring about him when he panicked with the sirens. She ended up with… nothing.

She *almost* wished Mark had never even come to Moonbeam. Almost.

CHAPTER 22

M ark tossed and turned all night. Flashes of the evening crept into his dreams. In his dreams, Collette laughed at him. The server at Jimmy's laughed at him. He woke up twisted in the sheets, knowing Collette hadn't really laughed at him. But when he fell back asleep, she was still there laughing.

He finally gave up when light began to filter into the cottage and got up and dressed. He slipped out into the quietness of early morning and walked to the beach. The beach where just the other night he'd sat with Collette, feeling connected to her. That was before he made such a fool of himself. Before it was obvious that his silly thoughts that maybe, just maybe, there could be something between them were pure nonsense.

When he turned left, he saw Rose sitting near the water. Maybe he should just turn around and head in the other direction. He wasn't sure he was fit for company right now. Too late. She saw him and waved.

He jogged over to her.

"Morning, Mark. Want to join me?"

"I won't be very good company. I'm kind of out of sorts this morning."

"Want to talk about it? Sometimes that helps."

He debated talking to her. She was right. Sometimes it did help to talk. But he couldn't relive last night. "I think this is just something I need to work out on my own." And he'd worked it out. He'd just do everything to avoid Collette, then head back home. Forget everything that had happened in Moonbeam. He was even tempted to head back early. What in the world would he do with the rest of his time here in town?

"Well, I'm a good listener if you change your mind."

He nodded.

"So, what are your plans for today?"

He shrugged. "I don't really have any."

"Would you like to help me work on the town auction? The auction is to benefit the school's library. They don't really get the funding they need to keep it up to date with the books they need. Anyway, Violet is in charge of it. She wanted to do something to give back to the community. But now she's got Evelyn and Rob's wedding to deal with."

Books. Everything was about books here in Moonbeam. But he didn't have any plans. He should help Rose. It would keep him busy. "I could help you out." It wasn't like he had anything else to do. Except for avoiding Collette, of course.

"Great. The auction items are in the school gym. We need to get them sorted and put in the storeroom until the auction. It's in two weeks. They'll need to use the gym tomorrow for school. You don't have to work the whole day. Any help you can give will be great. Violet had some baskets that I'll decorate and combine some of the items."

"I won't be much good with that. I don't know anything about decorating baskets."

"Any help you can give will be great. There are boxes and boxes of donated items that need to be sorted through. Do you know where the high school is?"

"I do. Saw it when I was out exploring the town."

"Great. I'll see you sometime today, then. I really appreciate the help. Moonbeam has a way of making you want to help them out, doesn't it?"

It kind of did. He wanted to help with the auction. Help the town. And it wasn't even his town. As much as he'd enjoyed it, and even though it was now a town he wanted to escape from, he would like to help them. And avoid Collette. At least she'd be working today. If he stayed away from her shop, he'd steer clear of her. The school gym was as good a place as any.

Plus, he didn't really want to analyze why he needed to avoid Collette so much. The obvious reason was that he was embarrassed about last night. That everything last night brought home how different they were. From her talks with Heather of traveling the world, to her discussion of the book she was reading, to his stupid math error. Oh, and let's not forget him blurting out how much older she was than him.

"I'll see you later today." He smiled at Rose and headed down the beach, hoping a long walk would soothe his jangled nerves and chaotic thoughts. But no matter how long he walked—and he wandered for a few hours—the unrest clung to him.

He came back to the cottage, got cleaned up, then headed out to grab a late breakfast. In order to make sure he didn't run into Collette, since they had the uncanny ability to eat at the same place at the same time, he drove over to Belle Island and ate at a place called The Sweet Shoppe. Then he remembered that's where Collette had gotten the cookies for her sweet tea and cookies Saturday. She was everywhere, it seemed. He ignored that thought and had a delicious almond croissant, then still feeling hungry, he topped his meal off with a blueberry muffin. He finally drove back to Moonbeam to help Rose. A little after noon, he walked into the high school gym. Rose called out to him from where a half dozen tables were scattered around her and piles of boxes filled the area. He crossed over. "How can I help?"

"Could you start by opening up more boxes? Put the items on the table, and if it says who donated it, make a note and put it with the items."

"My writing is atrocious. You probably won't be able to read it."

"That's okay. Do your best."

He opened the first box from Delbert Hamilton. A vintage painting of Cabot Hotel. He carefully put it on the table and painstakingly printed out D-e-l-b-e-r-t—not a name he'd really heard before—then Hamilton. He leaned over to get the next box.

"Hi, Rose. I'm here to help."

He froze at the sound of Collette's voice. He straightened and turned around. And there she was. The last person he wanted to see.

She locked her gaze with his. "Oh. Mark. I didn't know you were going to be here."

"I saw him this morning on the beach and roped him into helping. Wasn't that nice of him?"

"Yes, it was." Collette walked up to the table, now avoiding looking at him.

"You want to help Mark unpack the

donations and label them? I'm trying to combine some of them into bundles."

"Sure. I can do that."

"I thought you worked Sunday afternoons." He stood holding a box.

"I usually do, but Jody is working for me today so I could help out with the auction. I'm a sucker for an auction benefiting anything to do with books." She turned her back on him.

Of course she was helping with the auction. He should have known that. She was always all about the books. He set the box on the table and opened it. The Complete Sherlock Holmes, volume one. He almost laughed out loud. Books were everywhere in this town. Even at an auction to raise money for books.

He tried talking to her again to cut through the tension. "Here's a book for the auction."

"Thanks." She set it on the table and walked away to another stack of boxes, far from the ones he was working on.

Okay, she didn't want to be around him. He got that. But wasn't that what he wanted anyway? To avoid her.

He busied himself combining donated items into logical groups. That seemed easy for him.

Kind of like doing the displays at the hardware shop. Logical. In order. Rose would put some in baskets, and some they boxed up to be set out together on the tables on auction night.

He said limited words to Collette as they worked side by side, and she wasn't her usual chatty self, either. Which was fine with him. Many awkward hours later, most of the items had been boxed up again with carefully lettered cards with the donors' names—written by Collette, not him—ready to be put out for the auction.

Rose stood, her hands on her hips. "I think that is enough work for today. Look at all we got done. Violet will be so pleased. She was really worried about the auction after she found out they'd be having a wedding at the cottages on Saturday."

"I'm glad we could help her. If she needs more help later, tell her to call me."

"I will. Thank you. You two should go run and get supper. You've been working here all day."

"Oh, no. I have to go by the shop. Make sure everything went okay today." Collette glanced over at him.

"Yes, I have to—" What in the world was he going to say? He had to go for a walk? Listen to another book? *Brilliant, Mark. Just brilliant.* "Uh, I should go, too."

"Okay, thanks, both of you." Rose picked up the last box.

They headed out together, though he lagged a bit behind her. She turned to him when they got outside. "I better go."

He nodded, and she turned and hurried off down the sidewalk. Away from him as if she were walking out of his life forever.

Pain seared through him, and loneliness settled in its wake. Why had he ever come to Moonbeam?

To her utter amazement and disappointment, tears sprang to the corners of Collette's eyes as she walked away from Mark. He'd hardly said a half dozen words to her over the hours they'd worked side by side. She got the message loud and clear. He wasn't interested in her. She got that.

Which was a good thing, because she wasn't

interested in him either. Not someone who was so unpredictable in how he was going to be, how he was going to act. She'd been right in her decision last night. Avoid him. So she hadn't been very friendly to him today, either.

Ignoring the tiny voice in the back of her mind that nagged at her to ask him to dinner, she strode down the sidewalk, passing the storefronts without really letting anything enter her consciousness. Concentrating on her steps. Her breaths. Willing the impending tears to go away.

This whole situation wasn't worth tears. She barely knew him. Oh, he might have caught her attention, and she briefly thought that maybe... maybe... But maybes were like if-onlys. If you lived your life with maybes and if-onlys you never moved forward. Never enjoyed the here and now. She'd never allowed herself to wallow in if-onlys and didn't plan on permitting herself to now.

She pushed into her beloved bookshop. "Jody, I'm back. Why don't you go ahead and go home? I'll close up."

Jody looked at her closely. "You okay?"

"Yes, I'm fine. Just a bit winded from a brisk

walk back to the shop." She turned her back on Jody and straightened a stack of books on the table.

"Okay, I'll see you on Tuesday morning," Jody said as she grabbed her things and headed out the door.

It was only fifteen minutes to closing. The shop was empty. Quiet. Which usually was a soothing place to be. But today she looked around the shop, wishing it were jammed full of customers. Noisy. Laughing. Talking. Not this cloying quietude.

She walked around, straightening shelves that didn't really need to be straightened, and watched the minutes on the clock tick away. Promptly at five, she flipped the sign to closed and walked up to her apartment. She didn't really want to be there alone, but she couldn't chance going to a restaurant and Mark showing up, which seemed to be at every meal in her life.

He'd be gone soon, though. So it wouldn't be so hard.

Or would it be harder?

CHAPTER 23

M ark went out for an early walk on the beach on Friday. So far, he'd been successful in avoiding Collette all week. Of course, he'd barely left his cottage. Listened to another audiobook. Drove to Belle Island twice for meals, just in case. Started making lists of things he wanted to get done at the hardware store when he got back. Mr. Mason had checked in on him and told him that he wasn't expected back at work until Tuesday. He was leaving Moonbeam early Monday. Only a few more days. He could do this.

And yet, he was feeling unsettled, and part of him wanted to just march into Collette's bookstore and see her. Talk to her. But what good would that do? It wouldn't change anything.

He reached the water's edge, and Rose was sitting in her usual spot on the beach. "Morning, Rose."

"Good morning. Join me? The sunrise is reflecting in the clouds. Isn't it beautiful?"

He glanced at the sky as he sank onto the sand beside her. "I admit I'm going to miss the sunrises and sunsets here in Moonbeam. I don't think I've ever seen so many in just a few weeks' time. I just don't ever look up when I'm at home. I'm always rushing around. To and from work."

"Maybe things will change now that you've seen the magic in the sky."

"Maybe."

"May I ask you something?" Rose looked at him.

"Sure."

"I thought I sensed some tension between you and Collette when you both were helping me with the auction."

He laughed. "Yes, there was some."

"What happened? If you don't mind me asking. I thought you two were friends."

"We are. Were." He closed his eyes, then opened them. "Things just got mixed up. Anyway, she's just so… so out of my league." There was that term again.

"What do you mean by that?"

"She's beautiful, a world traveler, well-read, smart. She's everything I'm not. I'm just a guy who works in a hardware store and has never even left the state of Florida."

"That doesn't make you any less of a wonderful person. Look how helpful you've been while you're here. The friends you've made."

"I could never be the kind of person she needs. The kind of man she needs. We're total opposites."

Rose looked at him thoughtfully. "You know, my Emmett and I, we were opposites. But I don't think there were ever two people more in love. He was my whole world, and I would have given up anything to be with him. We learned to appreciate the differences. He passed away this last year and I miss him so much."

"Oh, Rose. I'm sorry. That must be so hard." No wonder she sometimes had a sad look at the edges of her eyes.

"It is hard. But my time here in Moonbeam is helping me heal. But see, if I would have gone with the whole he's so different thing... I never would have had all those years with the most wonderful man. Sometimes we need to step out of our comfort zone." Rose stared at him for a moment. "Do you have feelings for her?"

"I... I do." There, he'd said it. Admitted it. Admitted it to himself and out loud.

"Then you should talk to her. Tell her how you feel."

"It's too late now. I've been a jerk to her. Ran out on her. Avoided her."

"And that can change now. You could go see her."

"But it wouldn't make any difference, really. I'm leaving in a few days."

"But you said you only lived a little over an hour away. That's not far."

"I just..." His mother's voice ricocheted through his mind. *You're not good enough for Collette. You're stupid.*

"Sometimes you just have to believe in yourself. You're a good man, Mark. Smart. Look how you organized so many of the auction items so quickly. Well-thought-out groupings of items. You're generous to give your time like that. You humor an old woman and sit out on the beach watching the sunrise with her. Any woman would be lucky to have you in their life."

He stared at her, listening to her words. The words he'd yearned to hear for the longest time. The words he'd hoped his mother would say to him someday. That he was a good man. Smart. That he was worth something. He swallowed hard and took Rose's hand in his. "Rose, you seem to know just what to say. I thank you for your kind words."

She smiled gently at him. "I only speak the truth. And now what you do with my advice? That's up to you."

It was up to him. Rose was right. But what did he want to do with her advice? Did he want to listen to it? Did he truly believe her words about him after years of hearing what a loser he was?

"Anyway, think about what I said. You

shouldn't pass up any chance for happiness that fate puts directly in your path."

"I'll think about it. I promise." He nodded and turned to look at the waves rolling to shore as if they'd help him sort it all out and give him the answers he was seeking.

CHAPTER 24

Rose watched as Mark headed back to his cottage. She should probably get up and go grab her morning coffee with Violet. But still, she sat and stared out at the waves. Gulls flew overhead, calling to each other. A blue heron dropped to the water's edge and stalked along in the foam on its long, spindly legs. Then, with a graceful swoop, it took off and flew down the shoreline.

"Did you see that one, Emmett? She was a beauty."

A light breeze lifted a lock of her hair, and she smiled again. Yes, he'd seen the heron.

Her Emmett loved the blue herons. Thought they were majestic. He'd always catch her attention and enthusiastically point when he saw one. She smiled at the memory.

Memories of when she first met Emmett flooded her mind. She'd been so young. Just nineteen when they met. He'd roared into town on a motorcycle. A loner. But he'd caught her eye with his unruly curls, lazy smile, and strikingly dark blue eyes. And his kindness.

That first day she'd been standing under a large live oak tree, worried about a stray kitten that had managed to climb up in the tree and was now crying. He'd climbed up that tree to save the kitten mewling high up in the branches and then climbed back down to place the kitten safely in her arms. Later that week, she ran into him at the town park, teaching a young boy how to ride his bicycle. They'd spoken for a bit. Then it seemed like fate was always putting him in her path.

They went out on a few dates. That was until her father forbade her from seeing him— not that it stopped her. She just hid it from her father. She was from a well-to-do family. She'd been given everything and never worked a day in her life. She was home for the summer from college. Emmett had dropped out of high school and had no real money to speak of.

But none of that mattered. They were so in love. They ran off and got married on her twentieth birthday, and she never returned to college. It was a bit over fifty years now. Her father disowned her, and she always swore she'd support her children in anything they wanted to do with anyone who made them happy. But she and Emmett had never been blessed with children.

Her father hadn't spoken to her for twenty-five years after she and Emmett married until he called her to his bedside as he was dying. He never apologized but had held her hand and said he loved her. Such a waste of so many years. But then, she could say the same about her and her sister…

Why could she give what she thought was sound advice to other people, but never take any herself?

Speaking of advice, she should probably mind her own business. She knew that. But something in her heart was urging her to go and talk to Collette. She wouldn't say what Mark had confided in her, but maybe Collette just needed a bit of gentle persuasion herself.

Collette looked up to see Rose entering the bookshop. "Why, hello, Rose. Did you finish your book already?"

Rose walked up to her. "No, not yet. I was just… ah, out for a walk. I thought I'd pop in and say hi."

"Would you like a cup of coffee?"

"That sounds wonderful."

"Jody, I'm going to take ten and chat with Rose. Call me if you need me." She poured them both coffee, and they went to sit in two easy chairs in the back of the store.

Rose settled back in her chair. "I just love this bookstore. It's so welcoming. You have a good selection of books and you always know just the right book to recommend to everyone."

"Thank you. The bookstore means everything to me."

"Everything?"

"I guess your work shouldn't be your whole world, but this store is kind of mine."

"And you like it that way?" Rose pinned her with a hard look.

"I… I think so. Well, I always thought so. But recently, I'm not so sure."

"What's changed?"

"Just… I wonder if some of my long-held beliefs are really how I feel anymore. Or how I *want* to feel anymore."

"Because of Mark?"

Her eyes widened. "How did you know?"

"I just thought there was something between you two. Then there… wasn't."

She let out a long breath of air. "I just never knew where I stood with him. Mixed signals. And I hate that. I've always avoided it. I want to know where I stand with someone I… that I care about." There. She'd said it. That she cared about Mark. Not that it had gotten her anywhere.

"Sometimes it takes a person a bit to sort out their feelings. They can give off a hot-cold vibe while they work it out."

"Maybe."

"So you do care about Mark?" Rose took a sip of her coffee.

"Way to ask the tough questions."

Rose smiled and shrugged. "You don't have to answer them."

"No, I don't mind. Yes, I do care about him. I've tried not to, but I do. It's just… I don't trust him not to…"

"To hurt you?"

"Yes, that. Or maybe he's not who I think he is. I don't know. I'm just confused about it all. But I'm not sure it matters. He's getting ready to leave town. I'm not sure if I'll ever see him again."

"You could always go find him. Talk to him."

"I'm not sure I have the words to explain to him how I feel. I'm not sure I *know* how I feel."

"Maybe if you talked to him, you could sort it out."

"Maybe."

"Sometimes when we avoid the hard stuff, we miss out on some delightful things in life." Rose took her last sip of coffee and set down the cup. "Anyway, I should run along now. I'm going to help Violet with a few things for Evelyn's wedding."

"I'll see you at the wedding tomorrow."

Rose disappeared from the store. Collette sat

and continued to sip her coffee, thinking about all Rose had said to her.

One thing Mark had done, which she guessed was good, if a bit painful. He'd made her examine her life. She spent so much time avoiding any relationships. Protecting herself. She hadn't gotten hurt again, but she was alone now because of those decisions. Did she want to be alone for the rest of her life? Was hiding from all the pain causing her to miss out on some wonderful times she could have like Rose said? Was she too old to change now?

So much to think over. And change was scary. Was she ready for change?

CHAPTER 25

"Quit fidgeting." Violet smacked Rob's arm. "I'm trying to get your tie straight."

"I can't ever make them look right." Rob frowned and fidgeted again.

"Hence the reason I'm redoing it. Now be still." She redid the tie and stepped back. "You look pretty good."

"Pretty good?"

"You know, for a brother." He actually looked strikingly handsome. And happy. He'd had a silly grin plastered on his face all day.

"How much longer?" He paced away from her and glanced out the window.

"Ten minutes."

"It seems like it's taking forever."

"Hey, I tried to keep you busy all day." And she had. Rob had helped her set up all the chairs and fix the arbor. He'd set up the cake table and Rose had decorated it, along with tying all the bows on the chairs. She could hardly remember what they'd done before Rose came to the cottages. She was always such a help, and she'd become a dear friend to them.

He paced from the window to the reception desk and back to the window. "Now?"

She laughed. "Come on. Let's go on outside. You're driving me crazy."

They stepped out onto the deck, and she turned to him. "You know you're one lucky guy, don't you?"

"I know it. I'm so lucky Evelyn said yes to marrying me."

"Yes, you are, but I meant you're so lucky because you have me as a sister." She grinned. "Come on. Let's get you up front to the arbor and wait for your bride. I take my responsibility of best man seriously."

She took his arm, and they walked out into the courtyard filled with family and friends. She looked up at her brother, beaming with happiness. So Rob had finally found his one and only. She couldn't be more pleased for him. Her heart filled with happiness for him. For both of them.

They went up by the arbor and stood there, side by side, waiting for Evelyn.

Evelyn stood in the green cottage at Blue Heron Cottages getting ready for her wedding. Violet had graciously offered the cottage to her to get ready. She should feel nervous, but she didn't. She felt calm. Confident. Sure of this decision. Glad they hadn't waited.

"Stand still. Let me get this button," Donna admonished her, then stepped back. "Oh, Evie. You look beautiful."

She looked at herself in the full-length mirror. The light lavender dress was lovely. Just the right amount of simple and fancy.

"Mom, you chose the perfect dress. It looks wonderful on you." Heather got up from the bed. "And those purple shoes are perfect."

She glanced down at them, wondering if they were a bit too much. But she'd fallen in love with them and they looked nice with the dress. And they were flats, so she didn't have to worry about walking in the uneven courtyard.

Violet had gotten lavender ribbon to tie bows on the chairs, and Heather had picked out a bouquet of white flowers mixed with tiny lavender ones for the cake table. Her wedding bouquet was a simple bunch of mixed white flowers with a lavender ribbon winding through it.

Melody had baked a wonderful cake and added real lavender sprigs to the top. She couldn't believe so much had come together so quickly this week. Though, she shouldn't be surprised. The Parker women knew how to make things happen.

"You did a great job with the makeup, Heather. I can hardly see my bruise." She looked closely in the mirror again.

"You look beautiful, Mom." Heather came over and hugged her.

"Are you ready for this?" Donna asked. "It's just about time to go out."

"I'm so ready. You'll need to let me take your arm, though. I don't want to use the crutches, and I'm still not totally steady on my feet."

"I've got you. Don't you worry about a thing."

Livy and Emily poked their heads in the door. "You guys set? I'll get the music started if you are," Livy said.

"Everyone is here." Emily danced around, whirling with energy. "And you look beautiful, Evelyn."

"Thanks, Emily."

"I think we're set," Donna said.

Livy and Emily left, and soon the music filtered into the cottage. Donna turned to her. "Let's do this."

They stepped out of the cottage and into the courtyard. Heather walked up the aisle first. Evelyn and Donna waited at the end of the aisle. She looked down the aisle and saw Rob standing there, looking impossibly handsome and very happy. Her heart fluttered in her chest and joy flooded through her. This is what she wanted. What she knew was right. Rob was the man she wanted to spend the rest of her life with. Facing life's challenges and sharing life's joys.

She nodded to Donna. "I'm ready."

She walked up the aisle on Donna's arm and took his hand as she reached the arbor. He leaned over close to her. "You look beautiful."

They said their vows in front of friends and family as the sky put on a fabulous display of color. And just like that, she was married. A grin spread across her cheeks as she walked back down the aisle on Rob's arm. Mrs. Bentley. She liked the sound of it.

They cut the cake and then mingled with the guests, trying to make sure they said hi to everyone. Her mother came up, dressed impeccably as usual, and hugged her. "You look lovely, Evelyn."

"Thanks, Mom."

"It was a great ceremony." Donna walked up and handed her a glass of champagne.

Heather came up beside her and wrapped an arm around her waist. "Mom, I couldn't be happier for you. Rob is a great guy."

"I am, aren't I?" Rob came walking up with Violet by his side and laughed.

"And modest." Violet shook her head. "Good luck with this guy, Evelyn. You're going to need it."

Evelyn looked at Rob and smiled, her heart swelling with emotion. "I won't need any luck, which is good, because I already used up all my luck finding Rob."

"I'm the lucky one." He leaned down and kissed her gently, then held up his glass of champagne. "To my beautiful bride."

"To Evelyn," the Parker women said in unison, raising their glasses as they gathered around her.

"To the last Parker woman to get married," Evelyn said, raising her glass.

"Hey, what about me?" Emily asked.

"You're way too young," Livy immediately answered. "To the Parker women."

They all clinked glasses, and she looked around at all their smiling faces. Her family. Her new husband. As far as she was concerned, life was absolutely perfect here in Moonbeam.

CHAPTER 26

The wedding had been lovely, and Collette was so happy for Evelyn and Rob. Evelyn was beaming with happiness, and all the Parker women were gathered around her. Collette decided she'd slip away from the festivities and take a walk on the beach. She was feeling strangely alone with all the family members and people with dates at the wedding. She'd come alone. Very alone.

She'd glanced over at Mark's cottage a few times but saw no sign of him. No lights on. Nothing. She hadn't seen him since working with him on the auction preparations. So many days without even a glimpse. But Rose's words from today kept echoing in her mind.

With one last look back at the happy couple, she crossed to the beach and kicked off her shoes, heading to the shoreline. The stars were twinkling overhead and moonlight danced across the waves. A perfect evening for a walk.

Then she saw him.

She was certain it was him. Mark. Sitting on the beach. Fate putting him in her path again.

She could just turn around and walk back to the reception. But he turned and saw her. Should she still walk away? He didn't wave to her or call her over. Her heart pounded as she wavered in indecision.

They both stood frozen in time. The seconds crawled by. Then he lifted a hand in a half-wave. What did that even mean?

Suddenly, she was done with it all. The questions. The uncertainty. She stalked across the distance and stood, hands on hips. "We should talk. Talk like adults. I have so many questions running through my mind. So many."

He stood up, wiping the sand from his shorts. "I—"

She held up a hand, stopping him before she lost her courage. "I feel like—unless I'm imagining the whole thing—that there's something between us." She couldn't believe she just gushed all that out. But she was finished with the uncertainty. The hot and cold with him. The not knowing. "Am I imagining that?"

He looked away for a moment, then back at her. "No, you're not imagining that," he said softly, the words a gentle caress. "And I was going to come find you after the wedding to talk to you."

"You were?" She eyed him closely, not quite believing him, but his face held a sincere look.

"I was. And you are right. There is something here." He motioned between the two of them.

"But you… you run hot and cold, Mark. I don't know where I stand with you."

"That's my fault. I'm just so…" He let out a long sigh. "I'm so unsure of myself. I don't really know how to do this. To have a relationship. I feel like…" He stopped for a moment. "I feel like I'm not good enough for you."

"You what?" She stared at him. "Why would you think that?"

"We're so different. You're smart and you travel and you read." He looked at her closely. "I don't read much. I'm dyslexic. I struggle with words. They jump around on the page. I do stupid things like get the numbers wrong when I total a bill. Like at Jimmy's."

"Being dyslexic doesn't mean you're not smart." She frowned. This explained a lot. His not reading much. How much he enjoyed the audiobooks so they could bring the story alive to him. Even the bill at dinner. "You're *not* stupid."

He shook his head. "My whole life, my mother said I was. So did my brother. I hear them chanting it in my head all the time. And I do make stupid mistakes."

She reached out and placed her hand on his arm. "We all make mistakes. It happens. Your mother and brother were wrong. And cruel. I'm sorry you went through that. Some people shouldn't be parents." She shook her head, her heart breaking for the little boy being told he was stupid. For the man who still believed those words.

"It's hard to get them out of my head. They are always there. Telling me what I'm doing wrong." The pain was clear in his eyes.

"We'll have to find a way to reprogram your brain, then."

"We?" He looked at her.

"We. If I have to repeat a million times how smart you are and… how wonderful you are."

Disbelief clouded his eyes. "But really. We're so different. I don't travel like you do. You own your own business. You're successful."

"None of those have anything to do with who a person really is. What kind of person they are."

"But you were avoiding me when we were helping Rose. Ignoring me. I thought for sure you'd just gotten tired of me. Figured me out."

She looked at him as sadness filled her. "Let me explain. Come, sit." They sat down beside each other on the sand. "I *was* avoiding you. I was having a hard time dealing with how you were acting. Sometimes you acted as if you liked me, sometimes as if I bothered you."

"It wasn't you." He looked at her intently. "It was me."

She nodded. "But let me explain my reaction. Years ago, I promised myself I would never be interested in anyone who wasn't one hundred percent interested in me in return. If I wasn't certain, I'd walk away. I'd never chase after someone and hope that they'd like me in return. I did that once, and it had terrible consequences."

He took her hand in his. "Go on."

She let out a long breath. "There was this man. I dated him for years. And this whole thing is so embarrassing and so cliché. He was a salesman and my town was in his territory. He was in town a week or so a month. We went out every time he came to town. I fell for him. Hard. Then sometimes he'd call and say he wasn't coming. But then, eventually, he'd be back in town, acting like I was the most important thing in his world. Buying me presents. Taking me out to expensive restaurants. He was fun and exciting and oh so handsome. I thought he was going to ask me to marry him."

He sat quietly, giving her time.

She paused, sorting her thoughts. Taking out her painful memories that she'd never shared with anyone. Not a soul. "Then one day a friend told me she'd been in another city. The one where he lived. She'd seen him with another woman… and a little boy. Turns out, he'd been married all those years I went out with him and I had no idea."

"Oh, I'm sorry." His eyes were filled with sympathy.

"I felt awful. I never would have been with a married man. But it gets worse." Her heart tightened at the memory.

He just nodded, letting her continue.

"I found out I was pregnant. I didn't know what to do, how I felt. My world tilted out of control."

He squeezed her hand.

"But then… I lost the baby. And I still, to this day, don't know how I truly felt. There was some relief. And I felt guilty about that. But also a deep sorrow for what I was missing. The chance to have a child. But a child with a man who was married? It was all so very horrible and so very sad."

"I'm sorry you went through all that."

"But I made up my mind to never be in that position again. I'm sure I've chased a number of would-be boyfriends away over the years, demanding they tell me how they felt. Prove themselves to me." She shrugged. "I'm still pretty messed up over that after all these years."

"So my wavering back and forth, it hit all your buttons, didn't it?"

"It did."

"It was all so fast for me. I didn't expect to…" He looked at her closely and took her other hand in his. "I didn't expect to fall for you. To care about you. You were an unexpected surprise on this trip. And I do care about you." His mouth curved into a small smile and his eyes twinkled. "Since you like to know how people feel about you, I thought it best to just come out and tell you."

Her heart hammered, and her pulse raced. "You care about me?"

"I do. And I'd like to see where this leads us. If you'll give me a second chance."

She looked up into his kind eyes and nodded slowly.

He reached over and pushed a lock of hair away from her forehead. "And another thing. Let's agree to talk things out. I'm not great about expressing my feelings. I'm so used to hiding things after years of being told to. But I'm willing to try with you."

And suddenly she was ready to take a chance again. Ready to try with Mark. Even if things weren't all neatly lined up and tied with a bow. Even if it was scary. Even if they both were still figuring out how they felt. This was enough for now.

"There's one more thing I think we should talk about." She looked over at him, a serious expression on her face.

"What's that?" He frowned, looking worried.

"I think we should discuss when you're going to kiss me."

"Oh, I have a definite answer for that." He leaned close and kissed her gently, wrapping a hand around the back of her neck, pulling her closer.

The ridiculous thought that fireworks were exploding above them slipped into the edges of her mind. He finally pulled away. "Look up."

And there were the fireworks sparkling in the sky. "I heard Rob had gotten fireworks to surprise Evelyn." He laughed. "Good timing, Rob."

"I thought they were just for us." She looked

up at the bright flashes in the sky, then back at him.

"Maybe they are." He leaned in and kissed her again.

And she swore her heart was exploding in fireworks at his kiss as he tenderly held her in his arms.

EPILOGUE

Mark had called her every day since he left Moonbeam, and they talked late into the night. He promised to come back and help with the auction, and she couldn't wait to see him again.

She stood in the gym beside Rose, helping set up the tables for the auction tonight. Nervous energy ran through her, and she checked her watch no less than a dozen times. What would it be like to see him again? Would she still feel that sudden flutter? Or would they fall into some kind of awkwardness? She just wanted to see him again. And not through the screen on her phone.

Suddenly, there he was, standing before her.

She hurried around the table and threw herself into his arms. "You're here."

He kissed her quickly, then smiled down at her. "I'm here. I told you'd I'd be here." He looked over her head. "Hey, Rose."

Rose grinned. "Hi, Mark. Welcome back to Moonbeam."

"No place I'd rather be."

The flutter was still there, and her heart did a little flip in her chest.

"Why don't you take Collette out for a little break? She's been working hard all day." Rose made a shooing motion.

"I should stay and help you finish."

"No, it's almost all ready. Come back about four? The auction and dinner start at five."

"We'll be back then to help you," Mark said as he threaded his arm around her waist.

They walked outside, and he paused, looking down at her. "I've missed you so much. Missed your smile. Missed everything about you. It's not the same just talking on the phone or video chatting."

A thrill ran through her. "I've missed you too. A lot."

They walked along the sidewalk, hand in

hand. Her hand felt so right wrapped in his. Her feet barely touched the sidewalk. "So, was Mr. Mason okay with you leaving again this weekend?"

"He was thrilled. Said that maybe I'd be taking regular days off now." He slowed his pace, then stopped. "And I saw Ian. He's doing better. He's back working at the hardware store. Brave kid. I still feel awful that he lost out on his chance of a scholarship to college, though."

"I'm glad you're feeling a little better about it all."

He started walking again. "Anyway, I was glad to come back and work at the auction. I hope you raise a ton of money for the high school library."

"Me too."

He suddenly stopped. "You know what? Why didn't I think of this sooner? I could hold an auction in Summerville to raise funds for Ian's college tuition. I know everyone in town would be eager to help."

"I told you that you were smart. That's a brilliant idea. I'll help you in any way I can."

"You'd come to Summerville to do that?"

She grinned. "That and to see you."

"Maybe we could coordinate our days off some." He eyed her.

"I think that is another brilliant idea." They walked over to the edge of the beach and stood under an old live oak tree that had been there for generations, withstanding any storm that tried to destroy it. "You think we can be like this tree?"

"What do you mean?" He looked up at the tree.

"You think we can withstand what life throws at us? Survive it all?"

He took her into his arms. "I have no doubt we can. I feel like I can survive anything with you at my side. I'm so thankful I found you. I don't want to mess this up."

"I feel the same way." She stood up on tiptoe and kissed him, certain she'd made the right choice. That even with any uncertainty about their future, she wanted to walk beside him while they figured it all out.

He looked up and laughed. "Where are the fireworks for this kiss?"

"Oh, they're here. Trust me. They're here." She laughed and kissed him again.

Dear Reader,

I hope you enjoyed this story. Are you ready for the next book in the series? Restaurant on the Wharf is book four.

As always, thank you for reading my stories.

Until next time,

Kay

Return to the Island - Book Five

Bungalow by the Bay - Book Six

Christmas Comes to Lighthouse Point - Book Seven

CHARMING INN ~ Return to Lighthouse Point

One Simple Wish - Book One

Two of a Kind - Book Two

Three Little Things - Book Three

Four Short Weeks - Book Four

Five Years or So - Book Five

Six Hours Away - Book Six

Charming Christmas - Book Seven

SWEET RIVER ~ THE SERIES

A Dream to Believe in - Book One

A Memory to Cherish - Book Two

A Song to Remember - Book Three

A Time to Forgive - Book Four

A Summer of Secrets - Book Five

A Moment in the Moonlight - Book Six

MOONBEAM BAY ~ THE SERIES

The Parker Women - Book One

The Parker Cafe - Book Two

A Heather Parker Original - Book Three

The Parker Family Secret - Book Four

Grace Parker's Peach Pie - Book Five

The Perks of Being a Parker - Book Six

BLUE HERON COTTAGES ~ THE SERIES

Memories of the Beach - Book One

Walks along the Shore - Book Two

Bookshop near the Coast - Book Three

Restaurant on the Wharf - Book Four

Plus more to come!

WIND CHIME BEACH ~ A stand-alone novel

INDIGO BAY ~ Save by getting Kay's complete collection of stories previously published separately in the multi-author Indigo Bay series. The three stories are all interconnected.

Sweet Days by the Bay - the collection

ABOUT THE AUTHOR

Kay Correll is a USA Today bestselling author of sweet, heartwarming stories that are a cross between women's fiction and contemporary romance. She is known for her charming small towns, quirky townsfolk, and the enduring strong friendships between the women in her books.

Kay splits her time between the Southwest coast of Florida and the Midwest of the U.S. and can often be found out and about with her camera, taking a myriad of photographs, often incorporating them into her book covers. When not lost in her writing or photography, she can be found spending time with her ever-supportive husband, knitting, or playing with her puppies - a cavalier who is too cute for his own good and a naughty but adorable Australian shepherd. Their five boys are all grown now and while she misses the rowdy boy-noise chaos, she is thoroughly enjoying her empty nest years.

Learn more about Kay and her books at kaycorrell.com

While you're there, sign up for her newsletter to hear about new releases, sales, and giveaways.

WHERE TO FIND ME:
kaycorrell.com
authorcontact@kaycorrell.com

Join my Facebook Reader Group. We have lots of fun and you'll hear about sales and new releases first!
www.facebook.com/groups/KayCorrell/

I love to hear from my readers. Feel free to contact me at authorcontact@kaycorrell.com

facebook.com/KayCorrellAuthor
instagram.com/kaycorrell
pinterest.com/kaycorrellauthor
amazon.com/author/kaycorrell
bookbub.com/authors/kay-correll